THE
CHANGELING

Zilpha Keatley Snyder

Illustrated by Alton Raible

A YEARLING BOOK

Published by
Dell Publishing Co., Inc.
1 Dag Hammarskjold Plaza
New York, New York 10017

Yearling ® TM 913705, Dell Publishing Co., Inc.

ISBN: 0-440-41200-5

Reprinted by arrangement with Atheneum Publishers
Printed in the United States of America
First printing—February 1986

10 9 8 7 6 5 4 3 2 1

CW

THE
CHANGELING

To changelings I have known

1

MARTHA ABBOTT WOKE UP ON THE SEVENTH DAY OF April and sat straight up in bed with her eyes wide open. That, in itself, was significant. As long as she could remember she had always awakened slowly and cautiously, testing yesterday gingerly with the tip of memory, before taking the plunge into cold bright consciousness. But on that April morning she had no choice. Something had reached deep into her dream and jolted her awake—and then quickly faded, leaving behind only four definite words. *Something's going to happen!*

Not that she hadn't had that feeling before—that knowing that something terribly good, or bad, was about to happen—but never anything so strong and certain. Never strong enough to shake her awake and then leave her holding her breath, paralyzed with expectation.

She was still sitting, staring, numb with wonder, when suddenly her eyes focused on the mirror across the room, and the spell was broken for the moment. After the fraction of a second it took to recognize herself, she laughed. There she was, stiff as a hinge, arms straight at her sides, long hair wisping across her face, and her eyes round and blank as two daisies. Blinking, she smiled, imagining daisy petal lashes, and climbed out of bed, almost forgetting about the warning.

But it came back, and it kept coming back. It would sneak out, sudden and stabbing, and then fade again quickly when Martha tried to hang on long enough to examine it. The second time was only a few minutes later, while she was brushing her hair by the window, and watching the sunlight turn the long straight strands from straw to gold. *Something's going to happen!* This time it shivered down her back, leaving a fading shadow that felt very much like fear.

It happened, next, on the way to school, Roosevelt High School where Martha was a Sophomore. She had just turned a corner when there on the sidewalk was a bird. It was a brown bird, a perfectly wild brown bird, but it went on sitting still while Martha bent down and picked it up. Of course, it did seem to be a very young bird, almost a baby, but it wasn't just that it was too young to fly. Because, after it sat

4

in Martha's hand for a moment, it flew away. With just a very gentle boost from Martha, it flew away to a low branch of a nearby tree. It sat on the low limb, looking down at Martha, blinking its round black eyes, and suddenly, there it was again. *Something's going to happen!*

Nothing very special occurred at school, but that was to be expected. School seldom had the right atmosphere for significant messages. But one thing did happen. During drama class, Rufus gave Martha a flower. Rufus, who sat next to Martha in drama, was a special friend, and actually the fact that he gave her a flower was not so unusual. He often brought her little things as a kind of joke—a crazy little toy, or something funny from the newspaper, or a flower.

It was the kind of flower, this time, that made it matter. For Rufus had dropped into her lap a dark pink blossom of oleander.

"That's oleander," Martha whispered.

"Oh yeah?" Rufus said. "You couldn't prove it by me. It's that stuff that grows down by the highway."

"It's poisonous," Martha said.

"It is?" Rufus said, almost out loud, reaching to take it back.

"But only if you eat it." Martha kept it closed in her hand.

"Well okay, don't eat it," Rufus said.

Martha nodded. She twirled the blossom in her fingers and leaned toward Rufus to whisper, "That's me all right, beautiful but deadly."

Rufus snorted, and then they both sobered because Miss Walters was frowning in their direction.

Of course, the "beautiful but deadly" part had only been kidding, but oleander had been *very* significant to Martha once, and Rufus couldn't possibly have known about it. Rufus was a city boy, and that was probably the reason he didn't even know that oleander was poisonous. But the reason he didn't know the rest of it, was simply that he hadn't known Martha long enough. Only since September, and now it was April, and during that time Martha had never told Rufus anything at all about oleander.

The final warning occurred while Martha was on her way home from school. In a way it was the strangest, although Martha didn't realize that until much later. It happened while Martha was waiting for the light to change at an intersection in front of the school. Suddenly a voice said, "Martha? Is it Martha Abbott?" and there in a dusty station wagon was Mrs. Smith.

In spite of her ordinary name, Mrs. Smith was one of the most extraordinary people Martha had ever known. To say that she was the wife of the man who owned the riding stables where Martha had once spent a great deal of time, didn't begin to explain who Mrs. Smith really was, or why she had been important to Martha. But all that had been several years before, and it was a long time since Martha had seen her.

"Is it really you?" Mrs. Smith called, and Martha ran out to the window of her car.

"It's Martha," she said. "Hi, Mrs. Smith." She stuck her head in the window and said it again. "Hi, Mrs. Smith."

Mrs. Smith had a strange way of looking at people, a deep concentrated look, as if she could see things other people missed.

"You've changed a great deal," she said.

"I know," Martha said. "I'm not so fat and ugly."

Mrs. Smith smiled. "You're very beautiful, but that's not what I meant. Have you heard anything from—" But the light changed, and Mrs. Smith motioned Martha away and said, "Scoot now. Call me someday," and Martha had to run back to the curb. She didn't really think anymore about the meeting until after dinner much later.

Dinner that night at number two Castle Court in Rosewood Manor Estates was just the same as always. Everyone was there, at least all of the Abbotts except Tom and Cath Abbott, Martha's older brother and sister, who were away at college. The Abbotts present, besides Martha, included her father, Thomas Abbott, Junior; her mother, Louise Abbott; and her grandmother, Adelaide Abbott. Thomas Abbott was a lawyer, of the kind that mostly defends businesses against taxes. Louise Abbott was a housewife and didn't work, but she kept almost busier than if she did—at things like volunteer jobs and golf and staying very beautiful.

7

Grandmother Abbott spent most of her time traveling and gardening and going to garden clubs, and she ordinarily only stayed at number two Castle Court during the best gardening months. The rest of the time her garden, which was very beautiful and elaborate, was Martha's responsibility.

The conversation that night followed the usual pattern. Martha's father talked about an especially difficult client, and her mother talked about her golf score, and Grandmother Abbott talked about the Hollandaise Sauce, which she had made herself because Martha's mother had been so late getting home. Martha, wearing her usual smoke screen smile, was not really listening, when suddenly one sentence ripped through the screen and whirled everything into chaos.

"Oh, by the way," her father said, "Joe Peters says the Carsons have shown up again. Joe was up in Edgeport today, and on his way back he saw them from the freeway. They're moving back into the old Montoya house again. I was beginning to think we'd seen the last of that bunch around here. How long has it been since they left the last time? Must be two or three years."

"Two years," a strange voice said, which Martha hardly recognized as her own. "A little more than two years." And even while she was answering, another part of her mind was thinking, "So that was it. So that was what was going to happen."

Martha's father looked at her as if it had just occurred to him that she might have a particular interest in what he had said. "You didn't hear from your friend, did you?" he asked. "Did she let you know she was coming back?"

"No," Martha said. "I didn't hear from her. Was Mr. Peters sure? How could he tell for sure it was the Carsons, all the way from the freeway? He couldn't recognize faces from there."

"No, I suppose not, but Joe said he saw a bunch of people unloading what looked like the same old red truck they used to drive. Besides, who else would live in that old shell of a house? It must have been the Carsons, all right."

"It must have been," Martha said to herself. "It must have been."

"Well," Martha's grandmother said, but not so much to Martha as to her mother, "I suppose now we'll be seeing a great deal of that Carson girl again. What was that child's name?"

There was an undercurrent in what Grandmother Abbott was saying, and everyone at the table knew what it was. She was saying that she had always advised against allowing Martha to spend so much time with the Carson girl. She was reminding them all of the things she had always said, but Martha, for one, didn't need to be reminded. She already remembered all the things Grandmother had said on the subject. Things like, "I can't understand why you permit it, Louise. It's not as if there weren't any other children

9

her age in the neighborhood. There's that lovely little Peters girl right next door, and the Sutter children just down the block. And it's not just the child's unfortunate background. It's more than that. There's a strangeness about her—"

Martha remembered hearing Grandmother Abbott say that more than once. "There's a strangeness about her. A strangeness—." Suddenly an interior explosion shook Martha so hard that her smoke screen smile was blown away and she had to bow her head quickly to hide her face. Staring down at her plate she tried to explore the damage and wound up lost in a rushing tide of memories. Above and around her the conversation went on as if from a great distance.

Dinner finally ended and Martha, having cleared the table, was free to leave. Her father had made his regular retreat to the study with the paper, and in the kitchen Louise and Adelaide's regular polite argument was covering such things as "proper companions" and "interfering in your children's lives." Martha took her warm car coat from the hall closet and went out the double front doors of number two Castle Court into the April evening.

Martha walked uphill against a soft April wind, toward the unsubdivided green at the top of Rosewood Hills. Castle Court, which was formed by a cul-de-sac at the end of Castle Drive, was at the very top of Rosewood Manor Estates, so Martha had only to walk through the vacant lot that separated the Abbotts' house from the Peters' next door, and she was on a narrow foot trail that left suburbia behind. The path climbed steeply, zig-zagging through deep spring grass, and passing outcroppings of jagged turreted rock and scattered oak trees and madrone. The sky was just beginning to turn pink with sunset, but Martha could probably have climbed the narrow trail almost as well in complete darkness. All the hundreds of times her feet had climbed that path, walked it, run it, skipped or slid or scampered it, had printed a pattern somewhere in her mind. And now her feet followed that pattern automatically while her mind raced ahead, and back, rushed forward excitedly—and stopped—looking back longingly at yesterday and the day before.

Almost at the ridge of Rosewood Hills the path passed a small grove of old trees known as Bent Oaks, but Martha went on, straight up to where the path topped the crest of the hill and started down the other side. There, at the highest point, you could see beyond the northern slope of Rosewood Hills and catch a glimpse of a huge old ruin of a house. Half buried in orchard, the Montoya house was further hidden by the dark sweeping shadow of the freeway, where it dropped on a high overpass, down from a deep cut in the Rosewood ridge to narrow away into the distance.

Where Martha stood she could just make out part of the roof and upper story of the house, but that was enough to tell her that it was true. The Carsons had come back. Light was glowing in some of the upper windows for the first time in more than two years.

For a long time Martha stood looking down the dark north side of the hill. Below her the path quickly disappeared in the shadow of oak trees, and further down she knew it wound tunnel-like, under heavy brush, and then through the old plum orchard until it reached the house. Martha had been down that path once—only once. All the other times she had waited, as she would wait tonight, at Bent Oaks Grove.

The wind at the crest was not very cold, but Martha found that she was shivering. She turned back, and a few yards down the hill she took the turnoff to Bent Oaks. The trees of the grove had grown up among a very large outcropping of jagged boulders, and the path entered between two turrets of stone, like a narrow gateway between tall towers.

Stepping back into Bent Oaks Grove was like stepping back through time—two years of it. It was a jarring step—like the one that surprises you at the bottom of a dark staircase, when you think you've already reached the floor. Martha stood stock still, while bits and pieces of shaken up memories whirled through her mind. Then she moved forward.

The grove closed around her. Growing so near the crest of the ridge, the old trees were exposed to the full force of the wind, so that they had been bent in

places almost to the ground. Some of the branches, leaning away from the wind, had grown in great rolling twists and curves only a few feet above the hillside. The huge gateway boulders on the downward side had caught years and years of dead leaves and eroded soil, until the floor of the grove had leveled. Scattered around this flat area, small outcroppings of rock jutted up to form almost perfect chairs and tables, or mysterious monoliths and sacred altars, depending on who was using them. On the upward slope, a dugout area under a slanting rock made a shelter, a wide and shallow cave, and inside there was a rough wooden floor raised about a foot above the ground like a stage. At the edge of the stage a narrow path through a crevice led upward steeply to a ledge above the cave.

Once on the ledge Martha stood for a moment before she turned to climb on up the hill. Then she scrambled over boulders and pushed her way through underbrush until she came to a place where a flat rock covered a small crevice. Pushing aside the rock she pulled out a rough wooden box. Inside the wooden box, wrapped in a faded mildewed quilt, was another box—a metal one this time, a fishing tackle box.

Taking the metal box with her, Martha climbed back down to the ledge and from there by the crevice stairway to the stage below. The hinges of the metal box were so crusted with rust that she had to hit them sharply with a stone before the lid would open —but when it did the past sprang out at Martha like the creatures from Pandora's box. Swarms and clouds of memories rushed upwards from every object her fingers touched.

There was a peacock feather, a small leather-covered notebook, a ring box holding an odd-shaped amber stone, a tiny silver bell, some matches and pieces of candle in a glass jar, two horsehair rings, one carved ivory chopstick, a small crumbling bouquet of dead flowers, a large crystal doorknob set in a base of clay, and a yellowed envelope containing a photograph.

It took a long time to lay each object and its memories back in place, and when she had finally finished, Martha closed the box and with it beside her, she sat down on the edge of the stage. She pulled her legs up under her skirt, wrapped her arms around her knees and began to wait.

As she waited she began to say, "Ivy, Ivy, Ivy," letting the sound blend into the rising voice of the night wind. It was not loud enough for a call, or even an exclamation. After a while it began to seem more like a question.

2

Ivy Carson was seven when she first came to Rosewood Hills. She was too little for seven and wispy thin, with a small dark face that triangled from high cheekbones to a pointed chin. There was really very little of her to notice, except for her hair and eyes. She had wild hair, thick and too curly and almost never combed. It foamed in tangled curls inches thick around her head, and usually halfway covered her face. She had a habit of sticking out her lower lip and blowing upward when she especially wanted to see something, to get the hair away from her eyes.

You noticed her eyes, too, right away, even though you could barely see them through the curly thicket of hair. They were strangely beautiful, huge and dark and set in a heavy fringe of lashes, like two great glowing jewels in a skimpy little setting.

The next thing you noticed was the way she moved, as if her bones were lighter than air, or as if she had somehow managed to get herself immune to the law of gravity. That was all you'd see unless you got to know her well, but then, you also discovered that Ivy was not afraid of anything—at least not anything that you'd expect when you were seven, like the dark, or high places, or dangerous people or monsters.

Martha Abbott, that same year, was a little fat for a seven-year-old, and her straight pale hair was cut very short, because she sometimes cried when it was combed. At home she had, for some time, been known as Marty Mouse, because her new front teeth were coming in too far out, and because she was *very* easy to frighten. At school Martha's classmates described her as "the quiet fat one," and her teacher said, "a sweet child but an awful daydreamer."

That year, in the second grade, Martha had already heard quite a bit about the Carsons. Everybody had. For one thing their names were often in the paper— but not in the society pages, where other names familiar to the Abbotts were sometimes mentioned. The Carsons were usually written about under such headings as YOUTH ARRESTED FOR BICYCLE THEFT or TEEN-AGE BURGLARY RING BOOKED. Parents in Rosewood Manor read the articles and shook their heads and asked their children if there were any Carsons in their rooms at school.

Most of the children who went to Rosewood School lived right in Rosewood Manor Estates, but not the Carsons, of course. The Carsons attended Rosewood when they lived, from time to time, on the north side of the hills in an old wreck of a house that was known as the Old Montoya Mansion. There was a New Montoya Mansion some miles away where the real Montoyas lived. The real Montoyas were what Grandmother Abbott called a "very old family." People said that the Old Mansion still belonged to the Montoyas, although they had left it long before when the freeway overpass was built almost over its roof. The shade trees and lawns and garages and stables had been torn out so that an orchard could be planted right up to its windowsills, but the house itself had been left standing. People said that was because poor Mrs. Carson had been a Montoya before she married, and even though she was what Grandmother Abbott called "a disgrace to her good name," the house had been left for her to use for as long as she lived. So the Carsons came and went, leaving Rosewood when the trouble they were always in got particularly bad— and coming back when things had blown over.

All the Carsons seemed to be forever in trouble, and it was possible to hear all sorts of rumors about what kind of trouble. Younger Rosewood kids liked to scare each other by guessing murder and kidnapping, and slightly older ones thought it might be smuggling or piracy. But when Martha asked her father about it, his answer wasn't quite that exciting.

Mr. Abbott said that Monty Carson seemed to have a weakness for dishonesty in a small way, and bad luck in a big way. Like marrying for money and then getting nothing but an old wreck of a house, or buying large quantities of merchandise at auctions or bankruptcy sales and then not being able to sell them. And once he had started tearing the insides out of the old mansion to turn it into a roadhouse, and after half the work was done he found he couldn't get a permit. Of course, it was true that Monty Carson had been in jail at least a couple of times, but Martha's father said he thought it was for bad debts or receiving stolen property, instead of the kinds of things the kids in Rosewood like to gossip about.

There were lots of Carson children, and there had been years when there seemed to be one in almost every grade at Rosewood School, but by the time Martha was in second grade, there was only one left— a boy named Jerry who was in fifth grade with Martha's brother, Tom.

But then one day, a few weeks after school started, there was a new girl in Martha's room, and it turned out that she was a Carson, too. Martha remembered exactly how it happened.

The class had been working quietly, heads down —it was Mrs. Morris's second grade, and Mrs. Morris was very particular about quietness—when suddenly the door opened and a loud clear voice said, "Hello, is this the second grade?" Everyone turned, and there stood a very small girl almost completely hidden under clothes and hair. A large dress, much too long and too wide, covered the newcomer almost from the ankles up to where the hair took over. Martha glanced at Mrs. Morris, expecting her to say something about using a "good classroom voice" because the voice from the door had been very loud; but Mrs. Morris must have been too startled, for once, to think about such things.

For an uncertain moment Mrs. Morris said nothing at all, and then she said, "Hello" in a surprised tone of voice. After another pause she asked, "Are you a Carson?" Mrs. Morris had been at Rosewood School a long time and she'd been through a lot of Carsons, but even so she seemed unsure. The new girl was dressed like a Carson, and she looked a little like one, too. All the Carsons were dark with heavy curly hair, high cheekbones and wide mouths. Most of them were also rather large and blunt looking. This new girl looked like a Carson seen through the wrong end of a telescope.

"I'm Ivy," the new girl said. "Ivy Carson."

"Are you sure you belong in this room, in second grade?" Mrs. Morris asked. She was probably thinking that since she had never seen Ivy at school before, she must be just beginning.

"Oh yes," Ivy said. "I'm all finished with first grade. I got first grade all learned down at Harley's

Crossing where I used to live with my Aunt Evaline. I usually live with my Aunt Evaline, only she's been sick so I came to live here 'til she's better. It's all written down about my school and everything on this paper."

She left the doorway and toured around the classroom on her way to the teacher's desk, looking around her at everything and even stopping to peer into the aquarium on the way. When she skipped up to the teacher's desk, Martha noticed, for the first time, Ivy's way of walking—a kind of weightless skimming, like a waterbug on the surface of a pond. While Mrs. Morris looked at her papers, Ivy turned around and looked at the other kids, and that impressed Martha, too. Martha could barely stand to face all those eyes at once, and she'd known most of them all her life. But the new girl looked around, blew the hair out of her eyes and smiled, and a lot of the class smiled back. In second grade some of the kids at Rosewood School could still enjoy the novelty of someone new and different without feeling they ought to punish them for it.

Martha didn't really meet Ivy right away, because when the teacher asked for a volunteer to show the new girl around, Martha was too shy to raise her hand; but after a while Ivy got around to discovering Martha. If she hadn't, they might never have gotten together, because in those days Martha would never have made the first move toward someone new.

It happened one day when Martha was late going out for recess. She started down an empty hallway, but when she turned the corner, there was Ivy sitting on a railing. She was talking to somebody—only there wasn't anybody there. Martha was embarrassed, and she just kept on walking, trying to pretend she hadn't noticed. She was almost close enough to touch when Ivy said, "Hi."

Martha jumped and mumbled and kept on walking. Ivy jumped down from the railing and ran after her.

"You're Martha," Ivy said.

Martha nodded. "How did you know?"

Ivy screwed up her face, eyes squeezed shut as if she were concentrating. "I think it just came to me." She opened her eyes. "I saw you, and I just thought 'there's Martha.' But maybe I heard the teacher say it. I'm Ivy."

"I know."

"Did you just hear me talking to someone?"

Martha nodded uncertainly. Ivy nodded back. Her eyes were dark gray, a kind of smoky black, and they stared without blinking. Martha started squirming. Finally Ivy said, "I was talking to Nicky. He's a friend of mine."

"Nicky?" Martha said, looking back along the hall.

"Well, his name is really Red Eagle, but I call him Nicky for short. He doesn't mind." She leaned forward and said more softly, "He's an Indian."

"An Indian?" Martha said in a squeaky voice, and she leaned around Ivy to look more carefully down the hall.

"Umhum," Ivy said. "But he's just a small one." She held out her hand. "About this big."

Martha looked carefully along the railing and up and down the empty corridor. There still wasn't anybody there, but she only nodded with a nervous smile.

"I've been bringing him to school with me because he's lonesome for Harley's Crossing. That's where I came from, too. But most of the time I don't talk to him when other people are around because they don't like it that they can't see him." Ivy's smile seemed to invite Martha to agree that that was a silly attitude.

"Can you see him?" Martha ventured cautiously.

Ivy looked down the railing. "Not exactly, right now. Sometimes I can, though. And I always know where he is, even when I can't see him."

Martha was beginning to have a strange excited feeling. "I—I—had a—uh, friend like that once," she said. "Only he was a lion. A great big lion, but very friendly. He used to sleep on my bed and walk around with me sometimes, mostly when it was dark. And I wasn't the least bit afraid of the dark when he was there."

Ivy stuck out her lip and blew upwards at her hair. Then she pushed it back with both hands, looking at Martha very hard.

"A lion," she said. "A lion is a very good thing to

have. You were lucky."

"I was lucky," Martha said. For just a moment she could remember so well that she could almost see the huge tawny face of her lion and feel his warm strong back under her hand, the way she used to feel it when she walked down the dark hall to the bathroom.

"Don't you ever see him anymore?" Ivy asked.

The lion faded, and Martha shrugged. "Oh well, I don't play that kind of game anymore."

"Why not?"

"Well, because I'm not afraid of the dark any-more—" Martha started, but then she stopped. After a moment she went on, "—at least, not very. Besides everybody teased me. And my mother told people about it at parties and things. She'd tell all about Marty's imaginary lion, and everyone would laugh. Things like that."

Ivy nodded. "What was his name—your lion?"

Martha hung her head. "It was—well, I just called him Lion."

"Okay," Ivy said. "Let's go see if you can find Lion again. Do you think you could if we both looked? Together?"

"I—I don't know," Martha said. Then something she'd been holding back wavered and slipped away. Feeling daring she said, "Maybe we could."

Ivy looked at Martha thoughtfully before she looked back down the hallway. Martha's eyes followed her gaze.

"There," Ivy said, "can you see Nicky now?"

Martha looked very carefully. "Maybe I can," she said slowly, and then louder, "Yes, I think I can, just a little. Does he have feathers?"

Ivy nodded. "I thought you could," she said.

Martha looked until he was very plain—a smallish Indian with feathers in his hair, sitting there quietly on the railing. "Hello Nicky," she said. Then she looked back at Ivy and—at the very same instant—they both laughed.

They started off then, looking for Lion, and afterwards Martha always remembered how excited she'd felt—as if she'd already found Lion again, or something even better.

3

From the time they went looking for Lion, Martha and Ivy were together a part of almost every day, in spite of the problems that arose. There were problems, and one of the first ones started because of Martha's sister, Catherine. That year, the year that Martha and Ivy were in second grade, Cath was in sixth grade, and Tom, Martha's brother, was in fifth. Cath Abbott was always the prettiest and smartest girl in her class, and she had dozens of friends, but not any best friend, so it was hard for her to understand about Martha and Ivy. She complained about them quite a bit that year.

Of course, Cath usually had something to complain about. The Abbotts sometimes joked about Cath being a complainer. Mr. Abbott said that Cath had a great many talents and complaining was certainly one of them. "And there's no use trying to shut her up until she's made her point," he said. "I guess she gets that from her lawyer father," he said, rumpling Cath's blond hair.

When Martha's father said that, her mother laughed coolly. "Well, I have to agree that a tendency to complain runs in that side of the family." Martha's father didn't laugh, and Martha had a notion that Grandmother Abbott wouldn't have laughed either if she'd been there.

Anyway, Martha and Ivy were one of Cath's favorite complaints for a while. For instance, one night at dinner, not too long after Martha and Ivy had met, Cath said, "Mom, I wish you'd do something about Martha. She and that friend of hers are always doing the nuttiest things at school. And everybody knows she's my sister. It's really embarrassing."

"What kind of things?" Mrs. Abbott asked.

"Well, today they were running up and down behind the backstop when the sixth grade was out for P.E., and they were jumping into the air and flapping their arms and making squeaking noises. I just about died. Everyone was laughing at them."

Everyone looked at Martha. Tom grinned at her and said, "What were you doing, Marty? Being Superman? I used to do that, Cath. I remember playing Superman with Clay Sutter when I was real little." He put out his arms and pretended to soar across the table. "Marty the Supermouse to the rescue," he said.

Cath grinned reluctantly, and asked, "What were you doing, Marty?"

"We were being the flying monkeys in the Wizard of Oz."

"See," Cath moaned. "Flying monkeys, right out in front of all my friends."

"Well, I think that's understandable," Mrs. Abbott said. "Children Martha's age often play make-believe games. After all she's only seven years old."

"Well I didn't," Cath said, "And the rest of the second grade doesn't do things like that. At least not right out in public. And Martha never did, either, until she started playing with that Ivy. Besides, Mom, that Ivy's a Carson, did you know that? I thought you and Dad didn't want us to play with those Carson kids."

Mom looked at Dad as if she wanted him to say something, but he only shrugged his shoulders and went on eating his dinner. Grandmother Abbott wasn't there, or she certainly would have had something to say. As it was, it was left up to Mom, and it was easy to see that what Dad wouldn't say, or the way he wouldn't say it made Mom angry. She smiled a hard sharp smile at Dad before she said, in her silkiest voice, "I didn't exactly say that, Cath dear. As I recall it was your *father*, and your grandmother, I might add, who thought it wasn't a good idea when Tom brought that big Carson boy home last year."

"Well, what do you think, Dad? About Martha and this Ivy Carson?"

Mr. Abbott sighed, "As I see it, Cath," he said, "this is a slightly different situation. The Carson boy was quite a bit older than Tom, and he'd been in some trouble around the neighborhood. Besides Tom had dozens of friends to choose from. He didn't need to choose a boy who—"

"Jerry's all right," Tom interrupted. "And he's in the same grade as I'm in."

"But he is older, dear," Mrs. Abbott said. "I don't really think a little girl like Ivy is anything to worry about. Besides I understand she lives with her aunt most of the time. It's quite likely she'll be going back to her aunt's soon, and the problem will solve itself."

"No, she's not! No she's not!" Martha yelled suddenly, and everyone stared at her in astonishment.

"Marty!" they said. "Don't speak to your mother in that tone of voice." "Marty. I'm amazed at you."

They were amazed because nobody yelled in the Abbott family—and especially not when they were fighting. The rest of the Abbotts fought quietly and politely by using words that said one thing and meant another. It was a dangerous game with rules that Martha could never understand, and so long before she had started crying instead.

She cried that day. When everyone turned on her in amazement, she burst into tears and dashed from the room, headed in the direction of her favorite crying-place. No one was in the least surprised at that.

In those days, Martha was known as a champion crybaby. She knew that a crybaby wasn't considered a good thing to be, but since she was one, she made the most of it. Not that she ever tried to start crying; but once she had gotten started, she put everything she had into it. The size and wetness of Marty's tears was a favorite family joke.

"Oh, oh, get out your water wings. There she goes again."

"Good night, Marty, what are you bawling for? I hardly touched you. Now cut it out before you drown yourself."

"Marty's crying again. Every hour on the hour. Just like Old Faithful."

Martha had begun by crying anytime and anyplace, but after everyone got to talking so much about it, she had taken to doing most of her crying in one particular place. That was in a small luggage closet behind a larger closet. Martha had discovered she could push a tunnel-like passage among stacks of suitcases, to a low spot under the eaves behind a large steamer trunk. After she'd padded the spot with a favorite old quilt, it made a safe and comfortable hideaway for crying or hiding.

After a while, of course, Cath had discovered the hideaway and told the rest of the family, and it became another family joke. "Marty's Mousehole" it was called. The rest of the Abbotts seemed to think it was just another of Marty's imaginative games, but it had never seemed like a game to Martha. As it turned out, that evening when Martha yelled at everyone before she started crying was just about the last time she ever used the Mousehole.

With Ivy around, Martha had less and less time for hiding and for crying. Ivy changed a lot of things for Martha, and time was one of the most important. Before Ivy came to Rosewood Hills, Martha had never paid much attention to time, because there was always more of it than she knew what to do with. All the rest of the Abbotts kept very careful track of time, and they were very particular about what they did with it. "No, I just don't have the *time* today," they would say, or "You know that Tuesdays at 3:00 is my *time* for such and such."

Martha didn't keep a schedule, but if she had there wouldn't have been much on it besides school, and perhaps working in Grandmother's garden. The other things Martha did, such as eating and sleeping and reading and daydreaming, were not the kinds of things that had to be scheduled, and there was always more than enough time to do them in.

But time began to seem much shorter after Ivy came. There was never enough of it for all the things they wanted to do.

4

THERE WAS NEVER ENOUGH TIME FOR MARTHA AND Ivy, and for a while places were a problem, too. When they first met, Ivy occasionally went home with Martha after school, but almost from the beginning there seemed to be trouble. There was, for example, the time they bathed the ducks.

It started on the way home from school one day when Ivy happened to find a broken twig shaped like a long thin slingshot.

"Look, Martha," she said. "It's a divining rod."

"A what?" Martha asked.

"A divining rod," Ivy said. "It's a special kind of magic stick. You hold it by the two short ends like this, and the other end points the way to water for a well or sometimes to treasure. My Aunt Evaline showed me how to do it." Ivy turned around in a circle, stopped for a moment, and then began to walk. "Come on," she called. "It's pointing."

Martha knew there wouldn't be anyone home at her house for quite a while to worry about where she was, so she ran after Ivy and the pointing stick. It led them across the highway and into the slough.

"It must be a water-finding one," Martha said. "There's lots of water down here."

"Well, maybe," Ivy said. "But I think it's another kind. Some of them find gold mines, or oil wells, or pirate treasure. Maybe there's a sunken treasure in the slough."

"Some kids say there's quicksand in the slough," Martha said uneasily. When they reached the reed-covered spongy ground she began to walk gingerly, gasping whenever her feet seemed to be sinking a little. Mud began to ooze up around the tops of her shoes. Ahead of her, Ivy walked lightly, holding the rod in front of her with both hands. They kept going on, through softer and stickier mud, until they reached the bank of the river that flowed through the center of the slough.

"Hey, look," Ivy said suddenly, and as Martha slogged up alongside she could see that everything was black. They had come onto a finger of stagnant back-water, branching off from the main course of the river, and the surface of the backwater was covered by a thick coating of heavy black oil. "It must be an

33

oil well finding rod. Look, we've discovered an oil well."

Martha had learned about discovering oil wells from a movie on T.V. "I guess that means we'll be millionaires," she said.

"I guess so," Ivy said, but then she added, "oh, oh, look." She was pointing to where a large rusty oil drum, at the edge of the bank, was oozing its contents onto the water.

"It probably just fell off one of those barges," Martha said.

Ivy nodded. "Oh, well," she said. "They probably wouldn't let us be millionaires, anyway. You probably have to have a license or something. Besides, I don't much like oil wells. I'd rather find a treasure."

Martha was just starting to agree when suddenly she said, "Oh," and jumped and grabbed Ivy so hard she almost made them both sit down in the mud. Something had moved in the reeds just a few inches from her foot.

That was how they found the ducks. There were seven of them, a mother, a father, and five partly-grown babies. They were all covered with a thick scum of oil, which made their feathers stick together so they couldn't fly. They all seemed very sick.

So Ivy caught the ducks, one by one, splashing after them through the mud and water, while Martha held the ones that were already caught. After the fourth one, she couldn't hold any more in her arms,

and she had to sit on the rest like a mother hen. That is, she didn't actually sit on them, but she squatted down so that her full skirt, a new wool skirt with lots of pleats, reached down to the ground. Packed in under the skirt, the oily ducks seemed to stick together and stop trying to get away.

When the last duck was caught, Martha and Ivy divided them up and put them into baskets, formed by holding up the fronts of their skirts, and started for Martha's house. On the way home Martha did notice the mud and the oil, and the smell, too; but Ivy kept saying that the ducks would die if the oil wasn't taken off right away, and that seemed much more important.

As soon as they reached number two Castle Court, they started scrubbing the ducks in the stationary tub in the laundry room. Almost immediately they discovered that it took two girls to hold and scrub one wild duck. Afterwards Martha could never quite remember how they happened to put the other six ducks in the wicker toy chest in her bedroom, except that the Abbotts' just didn't seem to have any very good place for storing oily ducks.

It wouldn't have been quite so bad if the ducks hadn't managed to bump the toy chest lid open—but unfortunately, they did. The result was pretty awful. Fifth grade boys aren't particularly sensitive to dirty messes; but when Tom, who was the next one home, looked into Martha's bedroom, he was very impressed.

When Martha opened the door to show him the nearly scrubbed ducks, the father duck was sitting on top of the dressing table mirror and two of the children were huddled in the middle of the bed. On the pale blue and white color scheme of Martha's bedroom, all the messes, oily and otherwise, showed up very plainly.

"Wow!" Tom said.

Suddenly Martha saw exactly what he meant. "Mom is going to be mad?" she asked.

"Wow!" Tom repeated. "You can say that again."

When Martha started to cry, Tom said, "Now stop that. That's not going to help. You and Ivy start catching them, and I'll go look for a box. The first thing you've got to do is take them back down to the slough, because if they're still here when Dad gets home, they're all going to wind up in the freezer."

That made Martha cry harder than ever. She could barely see for tears all the time she and Ivy were scrambling around the bedroom after the ducks. The ducks, once they were unoiled, seemed to be feeling much livelier; and catching them turned out to be a wet and messy free-for-all. But they were all safely in the box by the time the next Abbott got home. This time it was Cath.

For once, instead of teasing or complaining, Cath was very helpful. Perhaps it was because she had just gotten home from Girl Scouts and had a Good-Deed-for-the-Day on her mind, or it may just have been that one look at Martha and her bedroom, convinced her that Martha was in for enough trouble already. Anyway, whatever the reason, she had a very helpful idea.

Cath, who at times really seemed to know almost as much as she thought she did, pointed out that if the ducks were returned to the slough immediately they were sure to die.

"What did you wash them with?" she asked. When Martha said detergent, Cath said, "That's what I thought. You've removed all their natural oil, along with the black stuff. They won't be able to float. They'll just sink right down to the bottom and drown. I learned all about it when I earned my wildlife badge."

Then, even before Martha could start crying again, Cath went to the phone and called the Humane Society, and in a very short time an animal ambulance truck pulled up in front of the Abbott's house.

The truck driver was very sympathetic. He told Martha and Ivy that the ducks would be set free in a safe place as soon as their feathers had had time to regain their natural coating of oil. He put the ducks carefully in the back of the truck, and just before he drove off he said, "By the way, girls, have your folks seen you? I mean since you saved the ducks."

Martha shook her head.

"Well," the man said, "maybe it would be a good idea if you tried a little scrubbing on each other before they get home. You know what I mean?"

Martha looked at Ivy and down at herself. She

knew what the man meant, all right. She and Ivy were both wet and muddy and oily from one end to the other, and Ivy even had a couple of duck feathers caught in her curly hair. Ivy started laughing, and Martha managed a weak smile.

Ivy said it didn't matter about her. It was an old dress anyway and probably no one would even notice. So she went on home, and Martha went back to Cath for advice about her new skirt and her bedroom.

But this time Cath only said, "Ugh, that's your problem."

It was a problem all right. Several different cleaning establishments visited the Abbotts' house before everything was back to normal. And in the meantime Martha was forbidden to play with Ivy for a week.

"It's not that I blame Ivy for what happened," Martha's mother said. "After all, I don't suppose she's had much training about such things. But you certainly should have known better, Martha."

"I know better," Martha said. "I just wasn't thinking about it."

"Perhaps a week without Ivy will make you remember the next time."

"But I promise to remember," Martha begged. "I promise the next time I find an oily duck I'll remember not to put it in my bedroom."

But Martha's mother only shook her head. And even after the week was over, she always shook her head when she came home and found Ivy there with

Martha. Or if she didn't actually shake her head, she managed to look as if she were thinking about it.

So, the Abbotts' house wasn't too good a place for Martha and Ivy; and of course, the Carsons' house wasn't even a possibility. One time—just one time—Martha tried going home with Ivy. It was not long after the duck incident, and Martha's parents hadn't yet gotten around to forbidding her to go to the Carsons' house. They did forbid it soon afterwards, but by then it wasn't necessary. Because Martha had already been there and nothing could have made her go back.

She hadn't wanted to go, even that first time. But Ivy was on her way home just to get a rope they needed for a game they were playing, and she asked Martha to come along. "Come on with me, okay? We'll get the rope and come right back."

Martha stammered, not knowing what to say. She couldn't say no without telling Ivy that she was afraid. It was hard not to be afraid when all her life she'd been hearing stories and rumors about the Carsons and about the decaying old wreck of a house by the freeway. But how could she mention that to Ivy, who was a Carson?

"Okay?" Ivy said again, and Martha nodded, swallowing hard, and went along.

They came upon the house suddenly, breaking out from between the trees of the orchard straight into its spreading shadow. The shadow filled and overflowed a hardpacked area of orchard land that served as a back yard. The yard was cluttered with parts of cars and motorcycles, and stacks of boards and boxes. The orchard trees nearest the house seemed to be dead or dying, and the house itself had a diseased look, with its stained and crumbling walls and its broken windows like dead eyes.

Ivy led the way up a sagging flight of stairs to what seemed to be a back door. The first room they passed through was rather ordinary, at least it was recognizable as a kitchen. But beyond that there were no real rooms at all. In fact, it seemed less like a house than an immense dark cave, lit only by dim slits of light from far distant windows. In between—everywhere—near and far—there were only rough support posts. Stripped of the walls they had once supported, the ragged posts were hung with bits of plaster and wire and studded with protruding nails. Here and there were a few pieces of old furniture, and in several places Martha could see stacks of cardboard boxes and wooden packing cases. The roar of the freeway seemed to come from directly overhead, and from somewhere very near, came the steady crying of a baby.

They found the baby lying on a blanket near one of the windows. Boxes had been piled around it to form a playpen, but at the moment it didn't seem to be trying to get away. It was lying on its back and wailing steadily. When it saw Ivy, it sat up and smiled. Ivy leaned over the box and made strange noises at the baby, and the baby made noises back, smiling all over its round wet face. Martha never knew what to say to a baby, not having had much experience with them, but she could tell that this one and Ivy were well acquainted.

"Who's baby is that?" she asked.

"My mother's," Ivy said. "Her name is Josie."

"It seems to like you," Martha said.

"She likes to talk with me," Ivy said. "Babies like talking with people."

They left the baby, and Ivy led the way around stacks of boxes to a wide curving flight of stairs. The second floor was better. At least all the walls were still there, and it seemed more like a house. There was a wide hallway with many doors, and at the end of the hall a smaller staircase led to the third floor.

Ivy's room was on the third floor, and it was very small; but it had a balcony and a vine growing up around the window. The bed was only a camping cot, but there were pots of flowers and pictures from magazines pasted on the walls. Ivy was getting the rope out of the closet—her own rope that she had brought with her from Aunt Evaline's because a rope was such a handy thing to have—when suddenly the motor roar from the freeway seemed to get louder and closer. Looking down from the balcony, they saw a red truck bouncing over the dirt road that led to the house.

"Who's that?" Martha asked, feeling trapped and frightened.

"My father, I guess," Ivy said. "And maybe some of my brothers. Max, probably, and Randy and maybe Bill. We'd better go now."

On the way down the wide staircase to the main floor, they met a woman carrying a load of clothing. The woman was very thin and gray, and she smiled at them vaguely without saying a word. Ivy hurried Martha through the dim cavern of the ground floor and out the back door. The truck was parked not far away, and several people were standing near it. Most of them were big dark-haired men, and they were talking in loud rough voices.

As Martha and Ivy walked quickly and quietly across the yard, someone yelled at them, "Hey Ivy. Who you got there?" Martha looked around and saw that it was Jerry, the Carson boy who was in Tom's room at school. Ivy grabbed Martha's hand and went on walking. Then someone, Jerry probably, threw a beer can in their direction. It bounced near Martha's feet with a clang, and she jumped and made a funny frightened noise. Ivy scooped up the can and threw it back at Jerry; and as she and Martha reached the orchard, they could hear a roar of laughter following them as they ran.

Martha ran frantically, stumbling on the furrowed ground, as if all the horrors she had ever heard about that house and those people were close behind her. She ran and scrambled until exhaustion stopped her near the crest of the hill. When she dropped, panting, to the ground, Ivy sat down beside her.

Ivy glanced at Martha once or twice without saying anything. Martha panted and gasped and tried to smile. Ivy picked up a rock and tossed it carelessly in her hand. Finally she threw the rock hard against a tree and said, "That crummy Jerry!"

Neither of them mentioned the event after that day, but Ivy never asked Martha again, and certainly Martha never considered going back to the Montoya House. In fact, Martha thought about its existence as little as possible. When she thought of Ivy, she tried to think of her in other places, especially, in Bent Oaks Grove.

5

THE WIND AT BENT OAKS GROVE, SWEEPING ALMOST constantly over the crest of the hill, skimmed through the topmost branches of the old oaks with a sound like distant voices. The voices raved and moaned or breathed in brushy whispers, according to the mood of the weather; but either way they seemed to be speaking always of secrets and mysteries.

Bent Oaks Grove was a natural place for secrets; and as Martha and Ivy began spending more and more time there, secrets collected around every part of the grove. Each of the rocks and boulders, and many of the favorite climbing spots in the old trees, acquired secret names and sometimes long and complicated legends. There was, for example, the Fortune Table. The Fortune Table was a small smooth boulder top that almost always had a few fallen leaves on its surface. When you needed to have your fortune told, you swept away the leaves before you went away, and the next day you counted the ones that had fallen on the table during the night. An odd number meant NO, and an even number meant YES; no leaves at all meant that the table had refused to answer.

The Fortune Table, like most of the early secrets of Bent Oaks Grove, was based on suggestions made by Ivy. Ivy had an almost endless supply of information about magical things. In fact, she seemed to have an endless supply of information about almost everything—and nearly all of it, she said, she had heard from her Aunt Evaline.

It wasn't very long until Martha knew a great deal about Ivy's Aunt Evaline. She knew that Aunt Evaline was not really Ivy's aunt at all. She was actually a distant relative of Ivy's father, who lived in the little town where Ivy's father had grown up. Ivy's father had once owned an old house in Harley's Crossing and the Carsons went there from time to time. They had been there when Ivy was born, and afterwards her mother had been very sick and had had to go away for a long time to a hospital. It was then that Aunt Evaline had started taking care of Ivy, and by the time Ivy's mother got home everyone was used to the arrangement.

"Besides, I wanted to stay there," Ivy told Martha.

"You mean even after your mother got well?" Martha asked.

"No, I mean right away. As soon as Aunt Evaline took me home when I was two days old, I knew I wanted to stay there with her."

"That's silly," Martha said. "You were just a newborn baby. You can't remember when you were just a newborn baby."

"Why not?"

"Well, I don't know. But you just can't. Everybody says you can't."

"Well I can," Ivy said, and Martha believed her. She believed that Ivy had decided when she was two days old that she wanted to live with her Aunt Evaline, and she believed that Ivy's Aunt Evaline was probably the most wonderful person in the world, because Ivy said that, too.

But if Ivy talked a great deal about her Aunt Evaline, she talked very little about the rest of her family. Martha was curious about the Carsons, of course, particularly after the day she visited the old Montoya house, but right at first she didn't ask any questions.

There were so many things to be curious about, though, that not long after the visit she decided to ask at least one. She was sitting on a tree root at the time, watching Ivy who was getting ready to climb high into the tallest tree to hang a rope for a swing. Ivy was sitting on the ground taking off her shoes and stockings.

The question Martha had decided to ask seemed

safe enough—not anything that Ivy might not want to answer. Martha said, "Ahh," to get Ivy's attention and then asked, "That woman we met on the stairs at your house—who was that?"

"On the stairs?" Ivy said, standing up and tucking her skirt into the legs of her underpants. "Oh, that was my mother."

Martha was so surprised she forgot about politeness. "Your *mother?*" she said incredulously.

"Sure," Ivy said. "Why? Who did you think it was?"

"Well, I don't know," Martha said. "I just didn't think about it being your mother. I don't know why."

Ivy glanced at Martha who blushed, wondering if Ivy was thinking that she was thinking how different their mothers were. How different her own brightly beautiful mother was from the ghostly gray woman on the stairs.

"I guess it was because she didn't stop us to ask any questions," Martha said. "Like some mothers always ask where you've been and where you're going and everything. She didn't seem as—as curious as most mothers."

"I know," Ivy said. "I guess she's had so many kids she's used up most of her curiosity already." Ivy jerked a knot into one end of the rope. "Besides she drinks too much. Sometimes she hardly notices anything at all."

Martha tried not to be embarrassed, or at least not

to look as if she were, but Ivy didn't look at her anyway. She was busy putting her socks into her shoes and brushing the oak leaves off the seat of her dress. Martha felt she had to say something.

"Oh," she said, very unconcernedly, and then hastily, to change the subject. "Uh, how many kids are there? I mean how many kids does she have?"

Ivy stood very still for a moment as if she were thinking. Then she turned and looked at Martha with a strange expression. It was her eyes mostly. As if she were looking at Martha intently but with her mind on something else.

"Only seven Carsons," she said very distinctly. "Eight if you count me. But there are really only seven Carsons."

"What do—why don't—who—?" Martha stammered, overcome with such violent curiosity that the question kept tripping on itself. But Ivy had turned; and running to the trunk of the biggest tree, she started up it as quickly as a squirrel. Martha hurried after her, and when Ivy reached the first crotch, she leaned down and reached to grab Martha's hand to help her along up. Then Ivy went on, shinnying up a steep place that Martha was afraid to try.

When Ivy, carrying the rope in a coil around her shoulder, reached the spot she had in mind, Martha couldn't stand it any longer. Leaning out of her safe nest in the crotch of the tree she called up at Ivy, "Why don't you count? Why aren't you eight?"

"Ummmm," Ivy said, because she was using her teeth to hold one end of the rope, and then, "Because I'm not really. I'm really a changeling."

"A what?" Martha called, and the "what" turned into a squeak of terror, as above her, Ivy pulled herself off balance and almost fell. She teetered a moment and then steadied.

"A changeling!" she called down very clearly. "Don't you know what a changeling is?"

Martha admitted that she had no idea.

"Well, a changeling comes when some other creatures, gnomes or witches or fairies or trolls, steal a human baby and put one of their own babies in its place. And the human parents don't even know it's happened. At least, they don't usually suspect for years and years."

"Why not?" Martha found the idea so horribly fascinating she leaned out, craning her neck to look up at Ivy—almost forgetting how afraid she was of falling. "Can't they tell by looking at it?"

"No, because the supernatural people do it when the babies are just a few hours old—because that's the only time they can make the babies look just alike. Aunt Evaline says that in some countries, in places where they know about such things, they never leave a new baby alone for the first few days after it's born —so a changeling can't be left in its place."

"Do the parents ever find out—I mean, how do they find out if they've got a changeling or not?"

"Oh, later on, when they're almost grown, they start looking a little different sometimes. Especially if the real parents were goblins or trolls or something like that. And sometimes changelings start doing very strange things, or having strange powers. Like this one woman in England whose real parents were witches; she just got up one night and went off for a ride on a broom. Right up until then nobody knew she was a witch at all. She didn't even know it herself."

Martha stared, speechless, imagining an ordinary Englishwoman suddenly finding herself high in a black sky on a flying broom. She could almost feel exactly what a shock it would be. Coming back down to Bent Oaks and Ivy, she asked, "You—you don't think your real parents were witches, do you?"

"Oh no. Aunt Evaline and I think I might be a wood nymph or a water sprite or something like that. See, when I was born and my mother was so sick afterwards, with all those other kids and everything, nobody paid much attention to me at all, until I went to live with Aunt Evaline. And by then it was already too late. I suppose that was why I liked it so much right away at Aunt Evaline's. I didn't really belong where I was before, so no wonder I liked it better with her."

While Ivy was talking, she had finished tieing the last knot; and then sliding her legs over and down the dangling rope, she slid off the limb. She slid slowly down the twisting rope, approaching Martha's level and then dropping below it, so that her face spun in and out of sight. Watching Ivy floating, spinning downward, in and out of sunlight, no one could have doubted for a moment.

"Of course," Martha said to herself, "a changeling. That explains everything."

But by the time she had reached the ground, climbing slowly and carefully, feeling cautiously for the very safest handholds, Martha had decided to ask just one more question.

"Do *you* really believe it?" she asked. "About changelings and everything?"

"I believe in just about everything," Ivy said.

6

FINDING OUT THAT IVY WAS A CHANGELING WAS A great comfort to Martha, although she never understood exactly why. She only knew that she believed it in a different and fiercer way than she believed in most other things she couldn't exactly prove.

She believed in changelings more fiercely than she believed in reincarnation or divining rods, and even more than she believed in the Monster of Lake Onowora—and that was a great deal. Believing in the Monster was important because it was the Monster, and Ivy, who saved Martha from a whole lifetime of being a Brownie.

Martha became a Brownie not long after she and Ivy met, because being a Brownie is the first stage in becoming a Girl Scout, and the Abbott family had a long history of Girl Scouting. Martha's grandfather, Thomas Abbott the first, had given money to help build the Scout Cabin at Lake Onowora. Martha's grandmother and mother had both been Scout leaders in the past. And, of course, Cath was just about the champion Girl Scout of Rosewood Manor Estates. She had started out as a Brownie as soon as she was seven and gone all the way through. By sixth grade she already had medals on top of medals.

Martha, however, had known instinctively at a very early age that she was not cut out to be a Girl Scout. Of course, when Cath had started as a Brownie, Martha's mother had been the Brownie Leader, and perhaps that made a difference. Martha thought she would have liked that. It would be nice to have a definite appointment with your mother once a week, even if it had to be in uniform. As it was, by the time Martha was Brownie age, her mother was all involved in other important things, and there was a new leader named Mrs. Wonburg. Martha supposed that there were all sorts of ways to run a Brownie troop, but Mrs. Wonburg's troop was sort of a cross between an old ladies' sewing circle and boot camp for the Green Berets. Martha didn't like embroidering samplers with the Girl Scout laws any better than she liked taking nature walks in lockstep. Besides, Ivy was not a member.

But, of course, the Abbotts wouldn't hear of Martha's quitting, and so all that fall she daydreamed during meetings, puffed and staggered during calisthenics, and wandered off and got lost during hikes. Mrs. Wonburg reported to Mrs. Abbott that Martha was emotionally unsound, but that scouting would save her, if anything could.

So, on Thursdays, Mrs. Wonburg worked very hard at the salvation of Martha; but on all the other days there was Ivy. Fortunately, Martha's grandmother had decided to spend that winter in Florida, as she often did, and with all the other Abbotts on such full schedules, Martha had many unsupervised hours. Nearly all of those hours were spent with Ivy, at Bent Oaks or in other favorite places in the Rosewood Hills. One of the best of these was Lake Onowora.

Lake Onowora was a large county reservoir a few miles back along the ridge of Rosewood Hills, where the smaller Rosewood range ran into the coast range. By highway it was several miles to the lake and Onowora Park, but on the Ridge Trail it was less than a half hour's fast walk. On weekends when the weather was good, Martha and Ivy went there often on explorations. One day they took along a camera that Martha had inherited from Tom when he got a new one for his birthday. They took turns taking pictures all that day—along the trail, at the stables near the lake, on the steps of the Scout Cabin, and along the lake itself. When the pictures were developed, Martha and Ivy discovered the Monster.

Even when the picture was first developed, it was

a little blurry; but you could plainly make out the top of the smooth dark body and the strange sea horse head, rearing up out of the water of the lake. Ivy had heard, from Aunt Evaline of course, all about a wonderful monster who lived in a lake in Scotland, and who was famous all over the world. Ivy and Martha were sure that their monster was every bit as good. They decided, however, to keep it a secret until they could find some way to prove that they had seen him first and therefore he really belonged to them. At first they planned to set a trap.

For days they scouted the lake nearly every afternoon, lying in wait behind boulders and in the midst of prickly bushes. They saw any number of interesting things: wild deer coming down to drink, immense blurry tracks in a muddy bank near the skeleton of an unidentified animal, a bunch of little boys skinny-dipping—but nothing of the Monster himself.

But they had a clue that seemed helpful. The tracks had surely been made by the Monster, and it had probably killed and eaten the one-time owner of the skeleton. Therefore, they knew that their Monster was a meat-eating monster, and it would be necessary to use meat to bait their trap.

Their first plan was to dig a pit trap and cover it with twigs and grass. They borrowed a huge man-sized shovel, and took turns carrying it up the trail to the lake. There, choosing a likely spot in the main trail, they started to dig. But the soil around the lake

was clayey, and the shovel was hard to handle. They soon found that the only way two seven-year-old girls could drive it into the ground at all was for both of them to leap up onto the top of the blade at once, one on each side. That worked fairly well until Martha misjudged her leap and missed the blade, and the shovel tipped over on top of Ivy, whacking her on the side of the head.

After that, they decided that it probably wasn't necessary to catch the Monster itself, if they could only get absolute proof of its existence. Perhaps a closer and clearer photograph would do. Then the credit would be theirs, and somebody else could do the shovel work.

As time went by, the catching of the Monster, or at least the sighting of it, became almost an obsession with them. All sorts of other things were forgotten for the moment in the heat and excitement of the chase —even fear. Martha even found herself one day, when Ivy had gone back to Bent Oaks for something they'd forgotten there, all alone out on a limb. She had been left with the camera, astride a limb of a rather low tree, hanging directly above the spot where a pork chop, borrowed from the Abbott's deep freeze, hung temptingly on a string a little way above the ground.

Ivy had been gone for some time when it suddenly occurred to Martha that if the Monster was as big as Ivy sometimes said he would be, he might not be satisfied with one small pork chop—and the limb on which she was sitting was not so terribly high. Not long afterwards there was a splashing noise out in the lake; and Martha, suddenly amazingly improved as a tree climber, shinnied to the ground and was halfway down the Ridge Trail before she stopped to think. But when she did, she realized with pride that, considering everything, it was pretty amazing that she had been there at all.

The Monster continued to be camera-shy, and Martha and Ivy finally decided that he probably only came up on land during the night. They went so far as to discuss lying in wait for him at night, but Martha's newfound courage didn't stretch quite that far.

"Couldn't we tell someone else and get some help?" Martha suggested.

"Who?"

"Well, I don't know," Martha said. "Not my family I guess. They would just laugh and say things about Martha's imagination. Besides they're awful busy. We might tell the ranger, though."

"The ranger wouldn't believe us," Ivy said.

"How do you know he wouldn't? He seems like a nice man."

"I just know," Ivy said. "It's probably because of second sight. I have it sometimes."

"Second sight?" Martha asked.

"Sure," Ivy said. "Second sight is when you know something without knowing why you know it. It comes from inside instead of outside of you. That's why it's called second sight. First sight is outside. I have second sight about things sometimes."

"Does Aunt Evaline have second sight?" Martha asked. She was pretty sure what the answer would be, but she wanted to ask anyway. She liked the way Ivy looked when she talked about Aunt Evaline.

"Aunt Evaline even has third and fourth sight," Ivy said. "But anyway, I think we better think up some way to prove that there's a monster before we tell the ranger. If we could get some better footprints even."

"What if we made another pork chop trap and poured paint around it?" Martha said. Martha had once walked absentmindedly through a finger painting drying on the schoolroom floor. She had left very clear footprints across the schoolroom, and the teacher had had some very strong things to say about daydreamers who never knew where they were going. The memory was very clear in Martha's mind.

Ivy liked the idea, but she pointed out that the paint would sink into the ground if they poured it out ahead of time. The final solution was a pork chop baited trap rigged to a can of paint balanced on a tree limb overhead. The Monster would spill the paint as he ate the pork chop and tromp around in it while it was still fresh. They picked a good spot on the trail near the lake before they went home that night.

Martha, as usual, collected most of the supplies.

They needed a new pork chop—the hunt had dragged on for so long that it had become necessary to bury the old one—and a can of paint. The pork chop was no problem, but the only paint she could find was a small can of purple bicycle enamel that belonged to Tom. She smuggled the supplies to school on the day they were planning to set the paint trap, only to be struck down that very afternoon with chicken pox and sent home to spend a week in bed. The Carsons' phone was disconnected that month, as it often was, so Martha didn't know what Ivy decided to do about the Monster. That is, she didn't know until Thursday.

Thursday, of course, was Brownie afternoon. Safely home in bed, Martha was congratulating herself on the fact that even chicken pox had its good points, when Cath came home with a horrifying story. It seemed that Mrs. Wonburg, leading her troop on a hike to Onowora Park, had stepped on a pork chop and been struck above the left ear by a can of purple paint. Fortunately the can hadn't been large, but the enamel was "easy-spreading" and "fast-drying." Mrs. Wonburg was undoubtedly livid.

Martha immediately cast suspicion on herself by bursting into tears, and soon afterwards the can of paint was traced to the Abbotts through Tom's newly purple bicycle. And so Martha—who refused to implicate Ivy, even though, or maybe because the Abbotts were so sure that Ivy was largely to blame—was permanently expelled from the Brownies.

7

PAINTING MRS. WONBURG PUT AN END TO THE SEARCH for the Monster of Lake Onowora. But he was not forgotten. Martha and Ivy spoke of him often, and once or twice they left a small sacrificial offering from the Abbotts' freezer for him on the bank of the lake, near the spot where they had first seen his blurry footprints. But they no longer wanted to catch him or even to expose his presence to the rest of the world. It was really more exciting to keep him as a secret; and besides, Martha felt that letting him keep his freedom was the least that she could do for him. She owed him that much.

The first few days after the painting incident were very bad for Martha, while the disgrace of being expelled from Brownies hung heavy over her head. The whole family, except Tom who laughed and laughed, pelted her with questions heavy with bewilderment, concern, indignation and frustration.

"Why, in the name of sanity, would you do such a thing? Not to mention, how?"

"Yeah, Marty," Tom said under his breath. "How'd you do it? Show me how someday."

"What I can't understand," Cath said, "is how someone who almost flunked kindergarten because she couldn't learn to tie her own shoes, just two years later could build such a complicated rope snare. There's more to it than you're telling."

But because she was absolutely determined not to tell on Ivy, Martha didn't dare to offer any explanation at all. She never had been able to convince anybody with an outright lie, so her only defense was to fall back on her reputation as a crybaby. Her answer to every question was tears.

At least it worked. In the face of tears, the Abbotts, none of whom had cried for years and years, felt frustrated and helpless. Then they, being such busy people and having so many other pressing things to take care of, soon forgot about the purple paint problem.

But glad as she was to not be a Brownie, Martha knew, even then, that the Abbotts really meant well when they had enrolled her in the troop. In fact, they were always going out of their way to do something of the sort for her, because everyone was so certain that something needed to be done. The problem was knowing just what to do. With Cath it had been easy. Cath always knew exactly what she wanted, as well as how to get it, and the things she wanted were things the other Abbotts understood, like pretty clothes and a rumpus room in the basement where she could entertain her friends.

But with Martha, no one was ever sure what she wanted, particularly Martha herself. Like gardening. When she was practically a baby, someone, probably Grandmother Abbott, had decided that Martha loved to garden. So, for years and years Martha had worked in Grandmother's garden and got cute little gardening tools for her birthday; and all the time, Martha secretly wondered how she happened to like gardening at all. Particularly Grandmother's garden, where everything was so planned and perfect and it was so easy to step on something rare and expensive.

All the other Abbotts seemed to believe the gardening myth absolutely, but they obviously thought that Martha did need something more. Sometimes when she was talking to friends or relatives, Mrs. Abbott described Martha as a "real individualist" in a tone of voice that indicated it was a condition she approved of. But when only Abbotts were around, she often talked about the fact that Martha needed "bringing out." The Brownies had only been one attempt to "bring Martha out." Riding lessons were another.

The whole Abbott family was in on the decision to send Martha to riding school. It happened one night at the dinner table not long after the Brownie scandal had finally died down. Mrs. Abbott started the discussion by announcing that she had been talking to Maureen Peters and had heard that little Kelly Peters was starting dancing school. The Peters had lived next door to the Abbotts for as long as Martha could remember, and Kelly and Martha were almost the same age. Kelly was very cute and very dangerous. Ever since nursery school Kelly had played with Martha on the rare occasions when absolutely nobody better was available. The rest of the time, Martha was her favorite prey.

The Abbotts were always encouraging Martha to be best friends with Kelly. Martha would be in her room reading or something, and her mother would stick her head in the door and say, "Marty, sweetheart, it's too nice a day to spend alone in your room. Kelly and the little Sutter girl are playing hopscotch out on the sidewalk. Why don't you go out and play, too?"

Because Kelly looked so much like a spun-sugar angel and could act like one when she felt it was necessary, it was useless to try to explain that to approach Kelly when she already had someone to play with was as foolhardy as walking into a whirling buzz saw. If Martha were lucky, Kelly and whoever else was there would only whisper together, leaving her out of everything; but if Kelly was in top form, Martha would be greeted by a dimpled sneer and something like, "Look.

65

Old fatty squirrel face thinks we're going to let *her* play."

But no one would believe that, so she just said, "I don't feel like playing hopscotch today."

That night at dinner Mrs. Abbott said she thought it would be nice if Martha started dancing school with Kelly. Martha protested, but her mother insisted that she should not be so afraid to try something new, and that she would find it was lots of fun once she got started. Surprisingly it was Cath who came to the rescue.

Cath, of course, was already in dancing school and had been for years. With the authority of all that experience, she explained to her mother that not many girls started as young as seven, and the ones who did were always the ones with lots of *natural* talent. Martha suspected that Cath was really thinking that it would be embarrassing to have her chubby, awkward little sister galloping around looking ridiculous in a leotard, but Martha was grateful anyway. Martha's mother looked at Martha and sighed.

"Well, it does seem she ought to be involved in something with children her own age."

That was when Tom, who had taken riding lessons the year before, suggested that maybe Martha could learn to ride. "You'd like that wouldn't you, Marty?" he said. "You're always checking out all those books about horses."

"I don't know," Martha said, suddenly uncertain. It was true she had always loved horses, but from a safe distance. "I like to look at horses. But the ones they have at the Onowora Stables are all awfully big. Maybe I could learn somewhere where they have small ones for beginners."

"Small ones for beginners," Cath said, rolling up her eyes. "Next she'll be asking for one with training wheels."

But horses—with or without training wheels— sounded safer than dancing school with Kelly, so Martha agreed to try. And for once her mother was right. It wasn't so bad once she got started. Not that the classes themselves were so very great. Riding in formation around a ring with a lot of other kids all dressed alike in boots and jodhpurs wasn't terribly exciting—at least, not after the initial stage of acute terror was over. But there were compensations.

Martha had always been both fascinated and terrified by horses; and as her terror diminished, her fascination grew. Moreover, it turned out that Ivy loved horses, too; and since Martha had become a bonafide paying member of a riding class, the two felt welcome to just hang around the stables—visiting their favorite horses and breathing in the exciting horsey atmosphere. Sometimes, after Martha became more confident, they saved up their money, with Martha usually contributing the largest part, and rented two old gentle mares for a trail ride up in the hills.

Of course, Ivy had had no riding lessons, but she didn't seem to need any. She looked pretty funny in her cotton dress and sneakers instead of jodhpurs and boots, with her hair bouncing like black foam around her head; but that didn't change the fact that she was very much in command of the situation. The horses noticed right away. Things like confidence matter to horses, and they let you know if you don't have enough of it. Ivy never had any trouble. Martha's teacher was always saying that riding was simply a matter of confidence and balance, and Ivy just naturally seemed to have lots of both. But it did depress Martha just a little to see Ivy doing so easily what she herself had learned with such difficulty.

"You're better than I am already," Martha told Ivy a little sadly on their second or third trail ride.

But Ivy didn't take any credit. "I probably can't help it," she explained. "I suppose I was a cowboy in one of my reincarnations."

Martha wasn't too surprised. She already knew that Ivy had definitely been a dancer in another life. Reincarnation had been a new idea to Martha, but Ivy had learned all about it from Aunt Evaline, of course.

"Does your Aunt Evaline really believe all that, about reincarnation?" Martha had asked, but Ivy only shrugged.

"Believe it?" she said. "I don't know. She told me all about it, but she didn't mention about believing."

Even though Martha doubted that she herself had had much riding experience in another life, she gradually became a fairly good rider. And although she didn't make all the new horseback riding friends her mother had hoped for, Martha, herself was more than satisfied. She lost a little weight for one thing, and she had a lot of fun for another. Maybe the most important gain was a great deal of freedom.

The Abbotts were very enthusiastic about Martha's new interest in horses. Everybody knows that it's quite normal for little girls to go through a spell of being absolutely out of their minds about horses. And Martha had been such a strange child, with such odd problems, that it was obviously comforting to see her develop such an appropriate mania. Martha overheard her mother telling someone on the phone, "Oh, Martha? Well, we don't see too much of her around home these days. She's going through her horse period. Spends every waking hour at the stables. Oh yes, I quite agree. Very healthy." She sounded much more comfortable than she sometimes had when people asked about Martha. Martha was glad. And she was also glad that she was being allowed to spend so much time away from home with no questions asked. And since nobody asked, Martha didn't have to mention that Ivy was spending nearly every waking hour at the stables, too.

Rainy days, however, were a problem. That first winter with Ivy was a fairly dry one, but even so there were times when Martha was not allowed to go either to Bent Oaks Grove or to the stables for two or three days at a time. It was during one of those times that she learned just how incredibly fearless Ivy really was.

Late one Sunday night, when it had rained all weekend and Martha had not seen Ivy since Friday afternoon, Martha was getting ready for bed when she heard a noise outside her window. It was Ivy. Martha opened the window, and Ivy climbed in out of the dark and wet. She sat on the windowsill while Martha put her muddy shoes in the bathtub and brought her a big towel to catch the drips. Martha stared at Ivy, almost speechless with surprise, while Ivy sat down by the furnace outlet to dry herself.

"How did you get here?" Martha finally asked in a whisper, knowing but not believing it—because she knew for certain that nothing in the whole world could make her do it.

"The same way as always," Ivy said. "Over the trail."

"But it's dark out there, and raining," Martha said, but Ivy only shrugged. With her bushy black hair plastered to her head, she looked tinier than ever, as greatly reduced as a wet Persian kitten. Her eyes, in contrast, had grown even larger. Great dark eyes, full of liquid sparkles, like the eyes of a mermaid or a creature from another world. It occurred to Martha to wonder if Ivy's swimming eyes were full of rain— or tears.

"Were you really not at all afraid?" she asked.

Ivy buried her face in the thick towel for a moment before she answered. "There's worse things than dark," she said, almost in a whisper. Then she shrugged and blew upwards at her wet hair and said, "Besides, sometimes a changeling can see in the dark, just like a cat." Ivy spent most of that night with Martha, slipping out just at dawn.

Afterwards, that conversation and that night kept coming back to Martha; but she always tried not to think about what Ivy might have meant when she said, "there's worse things than dark."

8

SPRING CAME AND THE DAYS AT BENT OAKS GROVE and at the stables were longer and warmer. At the stables Martha and Ivy had come under the spell of a great love. Her name was Dolly, and she was a very special horse.

A little bit over thirty years old, Dolly still had the remnants of a noble beauty. Even though she had become a little bony and swaybacked, she still had a delicate high-browed face and wise and gentle eyes. She was dead safe with any rider. Not even the most terror-stricken and helpless beginner could tempt her into unruly behavior. As soon as she could decipher what the frozen or spastic little human on her back had in mind, she proceeded to carry out his wishes with a willing obedience that built up the confidence of even the most timid. She was perfectly agreeable to any suggestion—as long as it could be done at a very slow gait. Nothing in the world could make her go faster than a very relaxed trot.

Of course beginners adored her for the first few rides. But most of them, having learned skill and confidence from Dolly, also learned that Dolly was considered a baby's horse—and to be seen on her was enough to brand the rider as a tenderfoot. So they turned against her and gave their devotion to side-stepping, scatterbrained animals who snorted foolishly at shadows or blowing leaves. But not Martha and Ivy.

Martha realized that no horse but Dolly could have tamed the terror she had felt when she was first thrown carelessly into a saddle by Mr. Smith, who owned the stables. Ivy had other reasons for her love. Ivy claimed that Dolly was enchanted. She was probably not actually a horse at all.

No one worried if children went into Dolly's stall to play. Any kid who knew Dolly, knew that his own mother would sooner bite him or step on him than Dolly would. The way Dolly looked at you, even the way she moved when kids were around, made it plain that she thought of children as colt things, and herself as a kind of foster mother.

Martha and Ivy spent hours in Dolly's stall. They curried her and polished her hooves and braided her mane and tail. They hid bits of apple in their pockets, down their necks, in the tops of their socks and even

73

in their hair, and giggled madly while Dolly frisked them gently with a twitchy velvet nose. They kept her stall dazzlingly clean, and sometimes they sat in the sweet straw and talked for hours, leaning against Dolly's legs. As long as they kept the flies shooed away, she never so much as stomped a foot.

The day that Kevin Smith, the grandson of the owner of the stables, came to the stall door and stood watching them, they had been daydreaming there, as usual, under Dolly's placid gaze. They had been imagining the horses they would someday own, when they were old enough to have anything they wanted.

"I'll have an arab mare," Martha had said. "Sorrel with a flaxen mane and tail like Dolly, only she'll be younger and maybe just a little prancier."

Ivy's eyes were dreamy. "I'll have a coal black stallion," she said, "with a bright gold mane and tail."

Martha thought back over all the horse books she had known. "I don't think you can," she said. "I don't think there are any that color—black with gold manes and tails."

"How do you know?" Ivy asked.

"I just never heard of any," Martha said.

Ivy shrugged. "So?" she said. "That's no reason why I can't have one. Why can't I have something I never heard of?"

Martha was about to change her mare to gold with a black mane and tail, when Kevin's head appeared over the stall door. Martha poked Ivy to warn her, and they were quiet, watching Kevin warily.

"What you doing with that old mare?" Kevin asked.

"Nothing," Ivy said.

Kevin stared with an unfriendly grin for a minute, but as he turned away he said, "If she gets any thinner, my granddad's going to sell her to the dog food factory."

When he was gone, Martha and Ivy turned in unison to stare at Dolly, but she didn't seem to have heard. At least, she only went on eating, nuzzling out the best parts of the hay and shaking it gently before beginning to chew. Without a word, Ivy led the way out of the stall and together she and Martha went on a silent horror-stricken search for Mr. Smith.

When they found him, he would not deny that it was true. "It may not be for quite a while yet," he said. "But when a horse gets past a certain age, sometimes it gets to be impossible to keep any meat on their bones. No matter how much they eat, they just keep on getting thinner and thinner. You girls can understand that I can't have skinny old nags here at Onowora Stables. I can't have people saying that I don't take care of my horses—and that's what they would think."

Martha could only stare at Mr. Smith in silent misery while waves of hot tears ran down her face, but Ivy's dark eyes were dry and hooded like an angry cat's.

"Well, I think—I think you're a murderer!" she said, and grabbing Martha she jerked her away, and they ran. They went on running until they were half-way back to Bent Oaks on the ridge trail. Then they dropped flat on their backs in the grass beside the trail. While Martha sobbed, Ivy plotted; and by the time Martha had run out of tears, Ivy had a plan.

"We'll steal her," she said. Martha gasped and smiled, delighted and, of course, terrified.

"We'll steal her at night," Ivy said, "and take her to Bent Oaks Grove."

"But they'll find her there," Martha said. "Some-one will see her there and tell."

"We'll only leave her there until morning. We can get her as far as Bent Oaks Grove in the dark, and we'll tie her there and go home. Then early in the morning—it will have to be Saturday—we'll take her over the Ridge Trail and the High Trail into the Coast Range and let her go. There's lots of grass there, and she can live with the deer, and we'll go to see her now and then and take her oats and carrots."

It seemed like a lovely plan to Martha until she realized exactly what was going to be asked of her. She, Martha Abbott, who had always had to have all the lights on before she would go down the hall to the bathroom, was going to have to crawl out her window in the dark after everyone else was in bed and go up the hill to Bent Oaks all by herself.

"I don't know," she said. "I'll be scared."

"Being scared won't hurt you," Ivy said. "Why don't you bring Lion with you?"

"I don't know," Martha said. She hadn't needed Lion much lately, and she wasn't sure she could get him to come back. Besides she'd never taken Lion with her much further than down the hall—at least not in the dark. "I don't know if I can." Then she grinned faintly. "I think Lion will be scared, too."

Ivy laughed. "Okay," she said. "We'll do it. Okay?"

"Okay," Martha said weakly, wondering if she really meant it, and right up until Friday night at ten o'clock she wasn't sure. But when ten o'clock came she really did climb out her window into the pitch dark, with only Tom's flashlight, which she didn't even dare use until she was past the Peters' house and onto the open hillside. The flashlight made it easier to walk, but it didn't help the fear, since every kind of horror seem to crowd the dim edge of its narrow beam. By the time Martha reached Bent Oaks where Ivy was waiting, she was sick with fright and besides that she seemed to have been stricken dumb. Ivy had to shake her and pound her on the back for quite a while before her voice began to come back.

"Stop. Stop it. You're hurting me," she finally forced out in a kind of sizzle between her clenched teeth. She went on sizzling because she knew she didn't dare open her mouth any wider. She felt absolutely certain that once it got open, it would stay open, and all her fear would come out in a terrible, disgraceful howl, and probably her dinner along with it. "Come on," she hissed. "Let's do it quick because I think I'm going to be sick."

All the way down the trail to the stables they had to stop from time to time while Martha clutched her stomach with one hand and her mouth with the other and moaned. Whenever she did, Ivy would whisper, "Go ahead and get it over with. You'll feel better. Get it over with before we get to the stables." But Martha couldn't quite.

When they reached the stables, they skirted the yard to the rear and climbed the fence behind the buildings. Inside the stable everything was silent, except for the snuffle and bump of the horses; and dark, except for one dim bulb outside the front entrance. The girls made their way noiselessly down the sawdust-covered walkway between the stalls, to Dolly's door. As Ivy stood on tiptoe to reach the latch, Dolly softly nickered her surprise to see them there at such a strange hour. As soon as they were inside the stall, she nuzzled their faces happily in greeting, and suddenly overcome with the thought of what was going to happen to all of them if they were caught, Martha began to cry. She leaned on Dolly's manger, clutching her mouth while tears burned down across her hands.

Ivy, who was usually very patient with Martha's weeping, almost lost her temper. "Stop it, this minute," she said. "Here, you hold the flashlight while I

get the rope around her neck."

Martha managed to pull herself together, and the three of them made their way carefully through the stable, past the hitching racks, past the dark shadow of the Smiths' house, across the yard to the front gate —where suddenly the horrible truth dawned on them. The front gate was closed and locked. The girls had never seen it even closed before, and it had never occurred to them that it would be locked at night. Of course, they could easily climb the fence, but there was no way in the world to get Dolly to the other side. They were still staring at the lock in unbelieving terror when the floodlights went on in the stable yard, and there was Mr. Smith standing close behind them carrying a gun.

Startled by the lights and the sudden appearance of Mr. Smith, Dolly sidestepped quickly, and her hoof came down on Ivy's toes. Ivy screamed in pain, and that was the last straw. Martha's stomach did what it had been threatening to do all evening. The next time Martha looked at Mr. Smith, the gun had disappeared. He'd probably realized that he had enough of an advantage without it.

Within a very few minutes, Dolly was back in her stall and Ivy and Martha were sitting in the kitchen of the Smiths' house. Ivy, still angry, beautifully silent, had her shoe off and was soaking her rapidly swelling foot in a pan of water. Martha sat beside her, pale green and saturated with tears.

Mrs. Smith, whom the girls had rarely seen before, and who never seemed to take much part in the horsey doings of the rest of the Smiths, was bustling around in a bright-colored robe, and across the room Mr. Smith sat at the kitchen table saying nothing at all. Once he got up and came over to look at Ivy's foot and agree with Mrs. Smith that it was not broken, only bruised. Then he went back to his chair.

Martha finally stopped crying, and her cheeks were just beginning to dry when she remembered something she'd heard about horse thieves. It hadn't occurred to her before that that's what they were—horse thieves! A new tidal wave of tears flooded her face, almost drowning her in their hot flow.

"Now, now," Mrs. Smith said. "You've got to stop that. It's not so bad as all that."

Martha mopped at her sopping face and gasped, "Do—do—they hang you if you're only eight years old?"

"Oh, you poor little thing," Mrs. Smith said, hugging Martha's bowed head up against her. Then she turned to her husband and said, "Dan, what on earth is behind all this?"

Ivy spoke then for the first time since they'd been brought into the house. "You mean you don't know what he's going to do to Dolly?" she said. "That he's going to send her away to be killed?"

"Dan?" Mrs. Smith said in a small, questioning voice.

"Could you come in the other room a minute, Lil," Mr. Smith said. "I'd like to talk to you."

The Smiths both went out, and Ivy turned to Martha. "Do you want to run for it?" she asked. "I can't, but you could go right out the back door and run home."

"No, no," Martha whispered. "They know where I live, and besides I'm afraid to go over the trail alone."

When the Smiths came back into the room, they were both smiling, and everything was suddenly all right. They had decided to drive the girls most of the way home—and not insist on telling their parents—if the girls would in turn promise to give up horse stealing. And about Dolly, Mr. Smith said, "We've decided to just turn her out on the winter pasture for the rest of her life. I do sell a horse to the factories now and then, but Dolly's given more years of service than most. I guess she's earned a retirement."

Then, when it was over and Martha was jumping up and down with joy and relief, Ivy cried. Not buckets like Martha, but just two big tears that glittered in her eyes and turned her heavy eyelashes to thick shreds of wet satin. Ivy didn't say thank you with words the way Martha was doing. But as she was sitting on the floor putting her shoe back on over her swollen foot, she looked up at the Smiths and smiled; and Martha noticed that the Smiths stood perfectly still looking down at her for a long time, as if they had seen something very strange or beautiful.

9

ONE OF THE GOOD THINGS THAT CAME FROM SAVING Dolly was getting to know Mrs. Smith. Martha and Ivy had scarcely seen her before the night of the kidnapping. They had caught glimpses of her once or twice in the stable, and once they had passed her walking on the trail carrying a metal tool chest and an easel. She was a small slender woman; and, although they knew she was a grandmother, she seemed to be of no particular age at all. She was a painter.

After the kidnapping incident, Mrs. Smith began talking to Martha and Ivy whenever they visited the stables, and very soon they were good friends. After a while they found out why Mrs. Smith took no part in the stable business. She told them she didn't really approve of renting horses as a way of earning a living.

Mrs. Smith had strange feelings about horses, at least strange for an adult. One day when Martha asked her if she liked horses she said, "I love some of them. Some of them I can't stand."

"Why?" was all that Martha could think to say, but Ivy went further.

"Which ones do you think are bad?"

"Well, the big gray, Matador, for instance," she said. "Matador is cruel. He'd be a killer except that he is also a coward."

By then Martha had thought of other questions, but Ivy was nodding her head as if she understood perfectly and agreed. So Martha only asked, "What about Dolly? What do you think about her?"

"Dolly is beautiful," Mrs. Smith said.

Beautiful was a word that Mrs. Smith used a great deal, about a great many things. Once she told Martha and Ivy that if they had to time to pose for her someday, she would like to paint their pictures. When Martha asked why, she smiled and said, "Because you two are very beautiful."

Martha was amazed. She knew that Mrs. Smith used the word beautiful a lot, but still it was a surprise to hear it used to describe Ivy and herself. Ivy often seemed beautiful to Martha, but she'd heard grown-ups refer to Ivy as "unkempt" or "pitiful looking"; and as for herself, Martha had always known she was the unbeautiful Abbott.

But the picture did turn out to be very beautiful.

They posed for it in the pasture, near the edge of the lake. Martha stood beside the trunk of a small tree, looking up and with both hands stretched upward on the trunk. Ivy was stretched out on a limb just over her head. Mrs. Smith had them pose for several minutes while she sketched in the picture, and then she let them go away while she painted for a long time. Finally they came back while she put in their faces and hands, which turned out to be just about all of them that showed.

Mrs. Smith had painted a great deal more tree into the picture than was really there. Limbs and branches came from everywhere filling most of the canvas with mysterious green and leafy swirls. Out of the sea of green only faces and hands stood out plainly, glowing with a strange light that was also faintly tinged with a bright soft green.

When Martha and Ivy were finally allowed to look at the finished picture, they were amazed and delighted.

"We *do* look beautiful, don't we?" Martha whispered to Ivy, and Ivy nodded.

"We look like we were part of the tree," she said. "I mean, as if we lived up there and never came down to earth."

"Exactly," Mrs. Smith said.

The game of the Tree People started soon after that, and probably the painting had something to do with it. But if the inspiration for the game came from the painting, the real beginning didn't come until one afternoon sometime later, halfway up one of the oak trees in Bent Oaks Grove.

Martha and Ivy had always played in the oak trees. They were perfect trees for climbing, with their wide heavy branches and the easy slope of many of their bent limbs. And, of course, Ivy was already a very practiced tree climber. Aunt Evaline's house in Harley's Crossing was right at the edge of a forest, and Ivy said that she had started climbing trees almost before she had learned to walk. Now, at Bent Oaks, she could walk up sloping branches standing erect, with her arms held out for balance and her bare feet sure and steady on the rough bark. Sometimes she even did a kind of dance on the wide lower branches, bending and swaying easily and smoothly with a control and balance that seemed almost magic to Martha.

Of course, Martha couldn't begin to do everything that Ivy did, but she kept trying, and little by little she improved. It became easier as she worked at it, and the fact that she had begun to lose weight helped some, too. Finally she could follow Ivy to most of the special places in the Bent Oaks. All the special places had names by then—The Lookout, Falcon's Roost, Far Tower, and the Doorway to Space.

The afternoon that the Tree People began, Martha was swinging in one of the rope swings when she looked up and saw Ivy walking down a limb towards her. She was barefooted and her skirt was tucked into the legs of her underpants as usual, but she had her sweater tied around her shoulders like a cape and her hair was full of leaves twisted into a green crown. But even without the costume, Martha would have known by her face that she was somebody else.

"Who are you?" Martha called.

"I am a princess from the Land of the Green Sky," Ivy said. "I have discovered the Doorway to Space, and any moment now I will be on the Treeway that leads to the planet Earth."

"At any moment" was a phrase that Ivy used a lot. She was always saying that "at any moment" this or that might be going to happen. But what Martha and Ivy didn't realize as they began to develop their knowledge of the marvelous Land of the Green Sky and the people who lived there, was that "at any moment" their time together was going to be over—for two long years.

One day Ivy didn't come to play at Bent Oaks when Martha expected her, and the next day at school Martha heard that the Carsons had gone away. And that was all—for two long years.

The two years when you are eight and nine are two of the longest years in anybody's life, and they were particularly long for Martha. She still rode, and Mrs. Smith went on being a very special friend; but at home, Martha went back to dead center. At least that's the way it seemed in comparison to the hurricane existence of the other Abbotts. All around Martha's quiet dead center of books and daydreams, went promotions to vice president, golf tournaments, projects, campaigns, and social events—along with daily flocks of older boys and girls, friends of Tom and Cath, trailing behind them noisy slip-streams of talk about dances, games, parties and the opposite sex.

Sometimes Martha made a new friend, but never one who was just right, or who lasted very long. She cried less, those two years, and the dark wasn't so frightening; but a lot of things that seemed as simple as breathing to other people, still seemed as far away as the stars for Martha.

The Abbott household was full of stars. Martha's mother and father had won things and led things and been the best at things, all their lives. Cath, of course, had always shone at everything—and in junior high she was more of a star than ever. She was chosen class president, won first prize in the science fair, and was even the first girl in her gang to get a figure. Tom, besides being absolutely everybody's friend and favorite person, was a star in little league, and then he was quarterback of the touch football team.

But even though Tom was just as much a star as the other Abbotts, he always seemed a little more reachable to Martha. There was one day, for instance, when Martha stumbled into Tom lying in the grass behind the garage, with his arms across his face. He looked strange, flushed and puffy. Martha asked him if he was all right.

"Sure," he said, turning his face away. "I feel great. Just great."

"You don't look very good," Martha said.

"Look Marty. There's nothing wrong with me."

Martha sat down in the grass beside Tom and waited. After a moment Tom looked at her and grinned a sour kind of grin and said, "That is, there's nothing wrong with me except I'm probably the world's worst quarterback. I threw a really stupid pass at the game today, and the coach yanked me out and yelled at me in front of everybody. And he kept me out all the rest of the game, too. And then on the way home Dad read me out all over again." Tom made a stern face and said, "If you'd just listened to what I've been telling you about that play, Son, that would never have happened."

Martha giggled at Tom's imitation, and Tom grinned back. He asked Martha what she was doing, and when she said she was just on her way to sit in the grass and read *Wind in the Willows* for the third time, Tom asked her if she'd like to play a game of *Monopoly*. Martha didn't think she liked *Monopoly* much, but she said okay. Tom and his friends had a *Monopoly* fad going and, considering the amount of time they'd been spending on it, Martha thought it must be better than it looked.

That day she had a run of beginner's luck and lit on all the right things. She could have absolutely wiped Tom out if she'd tried, but she didn't much want to. Taking someone's money and houses away seemed like an awful way to win. When Tom finally lit on her most expensive property she said, "Look, Tom. Let's pretend that I was out of town and I just asked you to stay there and take care of the hotel, and you didn't have to pay the rent."

But Tom laughed and said, "You are really crazy, Marty Mouse. This game is *Monopoly*, not Make-Believe. You have to stick to the rules or it spoils everything. Someday you're going to have to learn how to play some real games."

When Martha asked why, he laughed harder; but she really meant it. She really couldn't understand why it was more fun to always stick to somebody else's rules.

After Ivy had been gone almost a year, the Carsons came back to Rosewood Hills; but Ivy didn't come with them. Instead, Martha got a letter from Harley's Crossing. Aunt Evaline was better and back at home, and Ivy had gone to live with her again. Ivy never wrote to Martha while she was with her family. She never said why, but Martha suspected that her father wouldn't let her. When the Carsons left Rosewood Hills, they never left a forwarding address, and there were usually good reasons why they didn't want to be found for a while. But once Ivy was with Aunt Evaline, she wrote every now and then. Her letters were as strange as she was, with no beginnings and no ends, at least not the kind most people write. Usually they said things like:

Dear Martha. There is a nest under our table. We think that at least one of the eggs is going to be something very unusual. I will let you know if it does. LOVE—LOVE—LOVE ivy.

Martha thought about that one for a long time. She tried to picture a nest under the various tables in the Abbott house and finally decided it must be an outdoor table—Ivy had said that she and Aunt Evaline did a lot of things outdoors. But that still left a lot of questions unanswered; and they didn't get answered, because the next letter was about something else.

Hello. I am studying to be a dancer, again. At Last. I know I didn't finish being a dancer last time because I know I am still one inside. My teacher is very old and once she danced before a king. I will too, someday. LOVE— LOVE—LOVE ivy.

Then, at last, after Martha had already started the fifth grade, the phone rang and it was Ivy; she was back in Rosewood Hills.

10

Ivy was back because Aunt Evaline had been very sick again and had been sent away to a rest home. Ivy wanted to know if Martha could meet her in Bent Oaks Grove. It was a Saturday, so Martha said she was going for a walk and then she ran all the way to the grove. She reached the stone gate towers completely out of breath, but Ivy was there before her.

Ivy seemed hardly changed at all. Perhaps she was a little taller, and her hair was longer. Instead of flying loose, it was braided in one wide braid that hung down her back so far that she could sit on the end of it. But all around her face little wisps escaped, as wild as ever, making curly black petals for her dark flower face. She was still very thin.

She noticed that Martha was thinner, too, right

away. "You're much thinner," she said, "and you have bands on your teeth, and your hair is longer and yellower. When your mouth is shut, you look like a Viking Princess." Martha thought about that every time she looked in the mirror for a long time. No one had ever said anything so interesting about Martha's looks before.

"What was it like at Aunt Evaline's?" Martha asked.

"Just like always," Ivy said. "Except Aunt Evaline isn't very strong anymore. The woods are the same, and the river, and some of our friends. The best new thing was the dancing lessons." Ivy's face always seemed to be lit from inside when she talked about dancing. "There's this old lady in Harley's Crossing. Aunt Evaline has known her for years and years. Her name is Mrs. W., because nobody has time to say her whole name. Anyway, she was a very great ballet dancer when she was young. She's too old to even do much teaching, but because of being Aunt Evaline's friend, she started giving me lessons last year. So now I'm a dancer again."

"Again?" Martha asked.

"In this reincarnation," Ivy said. "Remember, I told you about how I knew I was one before."

"Oh, yes." Martha said. Then, after a while, she asked "Now that you're a dancer, are you a changeling anymore?" She was pretty sure what the answer would be, but it seemed important to hear Ivy say it.

93

Ivy said, "Don't be silly. You're either a change-ling or you're not." And Martha felt strangely re-lieved. She didn't know exactly why, but she knew that that was one thing she didn't want to change.

"What have you been doing?" Ivy asked.

"Not much," Martha said. "I still go to the stables quite a bit. Fifth grade is pretty good. I read a lot of books."

"Did you come here very much while I was gone?"

"No. I stopped and looked around sometimes on the way to the stables, but I didn't stay long. It's not so good alone."

"Alone?" Ivy said. "Did you forget about the Tree People?"

Martha almost had. After all, they had only begun to learn about the Tree People when Ivy went away. But now that Ivy was back, the whole thing started up again right where it left off.

The Tree People lived on another planet that they called the Land of the Green Sky. On their planet all of the land was covered by enormous trees that grew hundreds and hundreds of feet into the air; and the thick roots of the trees were woven together in a great solid floor that completely, or almost completely, cov-ered the ground. The Tree People were very beautiful and good. Their skin was pale green, and their hair was darker green and blossomed with flowers. They lived in softly rocking tree houses and traveled from place to place on highways that were the broad lower

94

branches of their forest world. They lived on fruits and nuts that grew everywhere, and their pets were tiny bright-colored monkeys and singing birds. Although the Tree People couldn't fly, the gravity was not very strong on their planet, and they could glide like blowing leaves from the higher levels to the lower ones.

However, the good and beautiful Tree People had very terrible enemies, who lived underground beneath the interwoven roots of the great trees. They were called the Lower Ones, and they were very cruel and ugly. Then, because of the death of one of the tree roots, a hole was formed in the wall between the two worlds, and the invasion of the Lower Ones began. Down in the great caves in which they lived, the Lower Ones had discovered the secrets of a powerful dark magic; and by using this magic they were able to turn some of their people into other forms. By doing this, they were sometimes able to kill or capture the leaders of the Tree People. In time the beautiful Land of the Green Sky could be conquered and ruled by the Lords of the Lower Level.

Martha and Ivy invented and played the Tree People game in many places, but most often up among the wide branches of the trees of Bent Oaks Grove. Sometimes they played themselves, Martha and Ivy, Earthlings who had discovered the Doorway to Space, and were able to travel to the Planet of the Green Sky to help the Tree People in their fight against the

Lower Ones. At other times they played the roles of such Tree People as Prince Willow, the handsome but weak prince, whose careless killing of a singing bird had caused all the trouble in the first place. Nothing was ever killed under the green sky, and there was a curse on bloodshedding, so that the blood of the dying bird, falling down onto the root of a tree had made it die, leaving an opening for the Lower Ones to enter the land.

There was also Princess Wisteria, the good green princess, and Lord Lilac, the kind but rather foolish advisor to the royal children. And then there were the Pretenders—Lord Hemlock and Queen Oleander and their daughter Princess Mistletoe—who were all, in reality, transformed Lower Ones. In fact, in the evil days after the death of the bird, the Land of the Green Sky was full of Pretenders—lovely green people who were hiding their true squat and scaly shapes behind the dark magic of the wizards of the Lower Lands. These Pretenders could only be detected by the fact that their beautiful emerald eyes were blank and color blind because they did not really use them for seeing, as true Tree People did. The Lower Ones saw only by means of an internal radar that perceived shapes and surfaces even in the dark, but could not see colors even in brightest daylight.

During hours and hours of playing in Bent Oaks Grove, Martha and Ivy developed the history of the Tree People and their cruel enemies, and played the parts of all the characters. They went through episode after episode involving attacks by the Lower Ones and near escapes by the royal family of the Tree People. Finally they played that Prince Willow and Princess Wisteria had escaped through the Doorway to Space and had become exiles on earth, where Martha and Ivy were helping them, though even on earth they were pursued by their evil enemies. Since weapons and violence were forbidden to Tree People, the only way to repel the attacks of the Lower Ones was by the use of superior magic. So it became necessary to constantly work at developing new spells and enchantments, and finding new charms and magical powers.

Once when things were most desperate, and Queen Oleander, who was by far the most dangerous of the Lower Ones, was about to discover the way to use the Space Channel to earth and arrive at the Doorway—just at that moment the Magic Wand was discovered.

The Wand had belonged to a magician of great power in the very distant past, but somehow it had been lost to him. When Martha and Ivy found the Wand, in an old trunk in the closet that had once been Martha's Mousehole, it had lost most of its power through being used for years and years as an ordinary useful object—an ivory chopstick, to be exact. But after an elaborate ceremony of purification and re-magicking, it regained all its strength; and for some time it was able to protect the exiled royalty in Bent

Oaks Grove by setting up a magical force field that prevented the entry of all evil creatures. But, like all the other magical solutions, it, too, was eventually made powerless by the magic of Queen Oleander.

She had, in her underground palace deep in the depths of the Lower Land, a Magic Fire Pit that burned with a gray flame. And by the light of the flame she was eventually able to discover evil enchantments strong enough to overpower nearly every form of good magic. That is, all except one. There was just one talisman whose magic was pure and strong enough to never be entirely conquered by Queen Oleander. That talisman was Josie.

Josie was Josie Carson, Ivy's little sister. When Ivy had been in Rosewood Hills before, Josie had been a little baby and Martha had only seen her once— the day she had paid her only visit to the Carsons' house. But during Ivy's second stay, Martha saw almost as much of Josie as she saw of Ivy.

By the time Ivy returned to Rosewood Hills, Josie had become a very lively three-year-old. She also became Ivy's responsibility. Mrs. Carson was sick a great deal that year. Ivy had told Martha that the reason her mother was sick was that she drank too much; but, whatever the reason, she was too sick most of the time to look after Josie. Since the only other girl in the Carson family was eighteen-year-old Brenda, who was much too busy with other things, most of Josie's care was given to Ivy. Most of the time Ivy's mother managed to stay well long enough to take care of Josie until Ivy came home from school, but just barely. As soon as Ivy got home, Josie was all hers.

At first Martha thought that having a three-year-old around all the time might ruin everything. However Ivy seemed to think it was all right. At least it didn't seem to be Josie that she minded. If there were things that Ivy was beginning to mind, that year, they were other things—and people.

Actually, Josie never was much trouble, and besides she turned out to be magic. Ivy said that most babies have secret powers. According to Aunt Evaline, people are always born with all kinds of magical abilities, but living in the world makes most of them lose the magic very soon. Josie still had some of hers.

Josie looked like a smaller rounder version of Ivy. Her black hair curled in short wild tangles all over her head, and her eyelashes were so long that they sometimes looked tangled, too. She had eyes that certainly looked magical, and it was perfectly plain that she could see people and things that no one else could see. She also remembered parts of a magical language, and it turned out that she was constantly surrounded by a field of invisible light that protected her and everyone near her from certain kinds of evil spells. She was constantly protecting the Prince and Princess of the Land of the Green Sky from Queen Oleander, and sometimes she protected Martha and Ivy from other sorts of evil.

11

Josie's magic worked in all sorts of ways—sometimes in ways that no one ever dreamed or expected. Like the time she had kept Martha from being exiled to Florida with her grandmother. It happened near the end of the summer when Martha and Ivy were between the fifth and the sixth grades.

A feast had been planned to celebrate the fact that Martha had finally learned to climb to a place high in the tree called Temple Tower. It was a fork between slender wavering limbs, very, very high above the ground, known as the Doorway. It was there one went to take off into the Space Channel. Before that time Martha had been forced to take off from a lower doorway, a specially developed concession to the fact that she tended to get dizzy in high places. So when she finally made it to the real doorway there was reason to celebrate.

The feast was to be held in the Falcon's Roost, since it was roomy enough to hold all three of them, and low enough so that Josie could be boosted and pulled up to join them. The food was to come from Martha's house. The menu was based on what Martha thought might be available and not too seriously missed, and since there would be quite a bit for one person to carry, Ivy was going to help. Fortunately, it was one of Grandmother Abbott's club days, and no one would be home.

Ivy still went home with Martha now and then, but almost always when no one else was there. They didn't have to explain why to each other or make excuses. They both just knew from experience that whenever it was brought to the adult Abbotts' attention that Martha was still spending a great deal of her time with Ivy Carson, the Abbotts started trying to find all sorts of other things for Martha to do. Right at that time it was particularly important not to stir things up, because one of Ivy's brothers had just been in the paper again, and as usual, not for anything good.

So, Martha and Ivy, and Josie, of course, entered the Abbotts' yard quickly by the back gate, in case Mrs. Peters, who was Mrs. Abbott's friend, and talked a lot, might be outside. They hurried through Grandmother Abbott's famous garden, towing Josie between them like a chubby glider not quite airborne. As they passed Grandmother Abbott's espaliered fruit trees, Ivy made a face. Martha knew why.

The first time Ivy had noticed the trees she had said, "What's wrong with those trees?"

"They're espaliered," Martha said. "My grandmother does it."

"I don't like it," Ivy had said. Martha had asked why, but even as she asked, she already knew. "Tieing a tree up like that and smashing it against a wall," Ivy said. "I just don't like it."

Inside the Abbotts' house Martha and Ivy went right to work hard-boiling eggs, making peanut butter and jam sandwiches, and squeezing lemons for lemonade. Ivy was up on the top step of the kitchen stool looking for paper cups, because Martha was sure she remembered seeing them somewhere up high, when Josie suddenly had to be taken on a quick trip to the bathroom. Martha and Josie were still in the bathroom, and Ivy was still going through the top shelves, when Grandmother Abbott swept into the kitchen, home early because she was sick with a headache and in a very bad mood. The picnic was off, Ivy and Josie were sent home, and Grandmother asked Martha a lot of suspicious questions.

That night when Martha's parents came home, Grandmother Abbott, without saying it in words, made it seem as if Ivy had been up on the stool looking for the family jewels or something like that. When

Martha tried to explain, her grandmother interrupted, "There, there, dear. Don't get so upset. No one is angry with you." And she gave the other Abbotts a look that said it was sad how easily the poor child was fooled by scheming people.

Martha went to bed that night feeling frustrated and worried. She had a terrible feeling that something was going to happen, and sure enough it did. A few days later her mother told her that Grandmother Abbott was planning another long visit to Florida, and this time she had offered to take Martha with her. There was a very nice private girls' school not far away from where they would be living, and Grandmother's new apartment had yard space where she and Martha could have a good time planting a really tropical garden.

Martha protested. She even came close to telling the truth—that she had always hated working in Grandmother's garden. But because Martha's love of gardening was such a long-standing family myth, she couldn't quite go that far. She did say, however, that she absolutely didn't want to go. But her mother only explained, as usual, that as soon as she got used to the idea she would be overjoyed.

"After all," she said, "it's not as if you really have been enjoying school here—the way Cath does, for instance. You know you've never taken a great interest in your studies, or even had a great many friends. I think it would be wonderful for you to have a chance to go to an exciting new place and a nice new school and get a brand new start."

"Go-to-Jail-go-directly-to-Jail-do-not-pass-go-do-not-collect-two-hundred-dollars," Martha murmured.

"What was that, dear?"

"Nothing," Martha said. She knew it was hopeless. They would close in around her gently and stickily, like a great inescapable spider web, until she stopped struggling.

There was nothing Ivy could do to help either. When Martha moaned to her about it, she only frowned and said, "You shouldn't go." There really wasn't very much more to say.

But one day, a couple of weeks before Martha was due to fly south with Grandmother Abbott, Josie's magic started to work. Martha and Ivy had been playing with Josie in the Falcon's Roost that day. Josie had been telling them about things that had happened to her before she was born. Josie remembered a lot of things that had happened to her that had certainly never happened to Josie Carson. Like being on a big boat out on the ocean. Ivy was sure that Josie had never been on a big boat, but Josie insisted that she had. "I did it a long time ago," she said, "before I was born." After Josie said that, Martha and Ivy looked at each other with raised eyebrows.

"Where did you live, Josie?" they asked. "You know, before you were Josie Carson."

"I lived in a little house," Josie said, "with a teddy

bear—and a vacuum cleaner."

"What other people lived in the house, Josie?" Ivy asked.

"A teddy bear and a vacuum cleaner," Josie said. She frowned at Ivy. "I said *before*," she said. She frowned harder and added, "I don't want to talk anymore." She snuggled into Martha's lap and put her face against Martha's. A minute later she said, "My face hurts." Martha noticed that her face was very hot; and when she and Ivy looked at Josie carefully, they could see that one of her round little cheeks was rounder than the other one.

So Josie had the mumps, and two weeks later just as the time came to take the plane to Florida with Grandmother, Martha had them, too. Because of social obligations, Grandmother Abbott had to go on without her; and afterwards the rest of the family gradually forgot their determination to pack Martha up and send her away.

Of course, as soon as it became pretty certain that Martha would not be sent to Florida, it was necessary to have a special ceremony at Bent Oaks Grove.

"We can call it the Ceremony to Honor Baby Magic," Ivy said. Martha wrinkled her nose and Ivy asked, "Why not?"

"I don't know. It sounds like a T.V. commercial —the Baby Magic part."

Ivy nodded. "Okay. How about Ceremony to Honor the Magic of New People?"

"That's perfect," Martha said. "New People Magic."

The New People Ceremony began by putting Josie in the middle of altar rock, where she sat with her legs straight out in front of her, sucking on her two middle fingers. They made a magic circle around her with sacred stones and feathers and put a wreath of leaves on her head. Then Martha and Ivy danced and chanted around the rock, making up the words to the chant as they went along. It was very long and complicated and beautiful, and afterwards they never could remember all the good things about it—but it was about the Wisdom of Newness, and the Secrets of Before. As they danced around, Josie didn't say anything at all, but every once in a while she took her fingers out of her mouth long enough to laugh.

The ceremony was almost over when Martha sensed, more than heard, something, and looked up quickly towards the lowest fork in Tower Tree, the spot she and Ivy called Falcon's Roost. She grabbed Ivy's arm and pointed, and sure enough, something bright colored was reflecting the leaf scattered sunlight. They ran to the trunk of the tree and looked up in time to see some long tanned legs starting down. The legs belonged to Cath Abbott.

Martha was, all at the same time, amazed, embarrassed and worried. She was amazed because it was probably the first time she had ever seen Cath all by herself—except when she was at home. Anywhere and

everywhere Cath went, as far as Martha knew, lots of other kids went too. So, to find Cath up a tree all alone was so astounding to Martha that, for a moment, she wasn't actually as embarrassed and worried as she might have been. Not even when she thought about the teasing she was surely going to get, and the remarks the rest of the Abbotts were going to make when Cath told them all about what she had seen.

But Cath wasn't laughing, at least not yet. She leaned against the trunk of Tower Tree and just looked at Martha and Ivy, smiling an odd smile. It took a moment for Martha to realize that the smile seemed odd because it was so completely ordinary—with no lifted eyebrow or curled lip or any of the other usual extras.

"Hi," Cath said. "I didn't mean to spy on you. I was just sitting up there—uh—thinking, before you came. So I just stayed there."

Martha and Ivy only nodded. Martha was remembering that she had recently heard Tom teasing Cath about somebody named Guy who had started going steady with somebody else. Martha wondered if maybe this Guy had been really important to Cath. Important enough to make her sit all afternoon in a tree by herself.

"I couldn't hear everything you said," Cath said, "but it sounded interesting. Is—is your little sister really magic, Ivy?"

Martha poked Ivy to warn her—and Ivy understood, but she only shrugged it off. "All babies are born with magic," Ivy said. "Babies are born knowing all sorts of magic stuff, until they start thinking separately and forget everything. That's what my Aunt Evaline says."

Cath grinned, "Ivy Carson, you are *crazy*," she said. But the way she said it was kind of respectful. "You kids are really far-out. That stuff you were singing sounded almost like some crazy poetry I had to read in English last year." Cath opened a small purse she was carrying and took out a little brush and began to brush her long swinging hair.

It was like Cath, Martha thought, to go off to be heartbroken all by herself, and take a makeup kit along. Finally Cath shook her smoothly perfect hair back from her smoothly perfect face and said to Martha, "It's getting late, Marty. I'll walk home with you."

Martha didn't really want to go with Cath, but she thought she'd better. If she walked home with Cath, she could probably find out a little more about what to expect—in the way of teasing and tattling. So she said good-bye and went off, leaving Ivy to put away the sacred objects and get Josie down off the altar where she had curled up and was about to go to sleep.

But Cath didn't do any teasing on the way home. Instead she was strangely quiet most of the time. Once she asked, "Do you and Ivy play that way a lot?"

"Like what?" Martha asked.

"Oh, you know. Imaginary stuff. Magic and all that?"

Watching Cath closely Martha answered, "Quite a bit."

"How do you think up all that stuff?" Cath said in a voice that sounded so honestly impressed Martha found herself answering frankly and enthusiastically.

"Ivy does most of it. Ivy is—well, she's great at imagining."

Cath didn't say anything more until they were almost home. Then she said, "I guess I just didn't know anybody like Ivy when I was your age."

It didn't seem possible to Martha that Cath Abbott could actually envy anybody, but the way she sounded it almost seemed as if that was what she was doing.

12

Martha and Ivy started the sixth grade together, and during that fall the games at Bent Oaks Grove and the history of the Tree People continued to grow. As time went by, both Martha and Ivy began to specialize in certain roles. Ivy especially liked to be the Princess Wisteria because the role required a lot of dancing; and Martha, to her own surprise, became an expert at being the wicked Queen Oleander. When she thought about it, it occurred to her that she liked being the wicked queen because the part gave her a chance to do all the shrieking and howling and ordering people around that she'd never dared to do in real life. But whatever the reasons, there were times when she amazed herself, and Ivy too, with a performance of really inspired wickedness.

As Queen Oleander became more powerful, she began to find ways to conquer one source of magical protection after another, and it became necessary for the other side to be always on the lookout for new magic charms or amulets. One search started after the Crystal Globe gave a timely warning of danger to come. When Ivy consulted the Globe, which had once been a large doorknob, it revealed that a new and particularly fiendish attack on the Earthlings and the Royal Family was about to take place. This time it was to be made by two million starving *sharls*. A sharl, Ivy explained, was a small spider-shaped animal with huge daggerish teeth. They usually lived like rats in the cave homes of the Lower Ones, but the wicked Queen Oleander had ordered a huge army of sharls to be trapped and starved into a terrible ferocity. And now she was preparing to release them through the Doorway into Bent Oaks Grove.

"What will we do, Earthling?" asked Martha who was being Princess Wisteria at the moment.

Ivy consulted the Globe again. "I'm not sure, Your Highness. The Crystal Globe has stopped talking. I think the wicked queen must be interfering with its magic. I see strange flashing lights and hear strange noises."

"Let me see," Martha said leaning over Ivy's shoulder. "It sounds like what my dad's electric razor does to the T.V."

But Ivy shoved her away. "Wait," she said. "I see

something. It's an eye. A Golden Eye." Martha tried again to see, and Ivy said, "There. It's gone again."

"What is the Golden Eye?"

"I don't know. We'll just have to find out. The Globe has gone dark again. You can see for yourself."

They both meditated for a while but with no results. Finally at the same moment they both looked at Josie who was sitting on the ground a few feet away.

"Josie," Ivy said, "how can we chase away the sharls?"

But Josie was playing with a safety pin and a piece of orange peel and she wouldn't pay any attention. She was making the safety pin talk to the orange peel.

"Josie," Martha said. "What would you do if a sharl was climbing up that rock beside you right this minute?"

Josie made the safety pin say to the orange peel, "If you shut your eyes, a sharl can't hurt you."

"Did you hear what she said?" Martha asked Ivy.

"Umm," Ivy said. "I think she means we have to find the Golden Eye and put it on the altar. Then when the sharls start coming, we all close our eyes— and then it happens."

"What happens?"

"The terrible power of the Golden Eye."

"But what is the Golden Eye?" Martha insisted.

"What is the Golden Eye?" Ivy asked Josie.

Josie put down the orange peel and put her finger on one eyelid. "Eye," she said.

"The *Golden* Eye," Martha said.

Josie sat very still with her finger still on her eye. Then she pointed off towards the southeast. "Way— way—over there," she said. So although it was already rather late in the day for beginning an expedition, they started out. Josie was given the magic chopstick wand to hold in both her fat little hands like a divining rod. Then they headed her in the direction in which she had pointed, and gave her a slight push. Martha and Ivy walked one on each side and a half step behind.

The journey began in the direction of the freeway and the overhead pedestrian walkway that crossed it. Josie walked very fast for someone with such short legs—and very purposefully as if she knew exactly where she was going. When they got to the walkway, Josie stomped up the stairs, two steps for each stair, and down the other side again. Then, she pointed the wand back the other way and started to climb back up.

"What's the matter?" Martha asked, thinking the wand had made a mistake. But Ivy only rolled her eyes and made an exasperated expression.

"She loves to climb over the walkway," she whispered. She went to Josie and turned her back around. "No!" she said. "Don't you remember? You are taking us to the Golden Eye."

Josie stuck out her lip and pointed, arms length. "The Golden Eye just went back," she said determinedly.

Martha giggled, and Ivy tried not to. "It did not," she said firmly. "You ought not to be thinking about climbing stairs when you're doing magic. Do you want me to let Martha carry the wand?"

Josie shook her head and turned around. The wand wiggled and pointed, and the expedition got back under way. They walked and walked further into the southern tip of the Rosewood Range than they had been before, until at last they came to a high iron fence.

It was an old fence, rusty and hung with dying vines, and beyond it lay what seemed to be the remains of a large garden. Through the fence, the dusty smell of dead plants and thirsty soil seemed to reach out and surround them.

Before long they were tiptoeing down a weed-choked dusty path that led upward under thinning trees. They wound their way up the hill until, coming out of the trees, they saw the charred and blackened ruin of a house. Staring at the dark and jagged silhouette, Martha felt her shoulders jerk in an involuntary shiver. She turned quickly to Ivy.

But Ivy was gone. Not really, but she might as well have been. She was standing perfectly still staring at the old house. There was a kind of blur about her, as if she had moved to a distance that had nothing to do with space.

"Ivy?" Martha said.

Ivy took a deep slow breath and turned to Martha smiling. "Let's go there," she said.

"Do you think we ought to?"

Ivy's only answer was to take Josie's hand and lead the way.

It had been a large and beautiful house, and it had burned a very long time before. The loose ashes had long since weathered away, and the fire's handiwork could only be seen on the charred edges of the walls, which rose in places several feet above the ground. Grass grew where floors had once been and a deep weed-grown pit marked the site of a large basement.

Martha and Ivy walked slowly all around the ruin. Josie ran ahead of them chattering away as usual, but Ivy was strangely quiet. They stopped, at last, near where some wide stone steps led up to nothing and sat down on the dry grass. Beside them was the blackened stump of what must have been a very large tree. Finally Ivy said, "It's *too* quiet. Have you noticed?"

"Too quiet?" Martha asked. She listened and the silence was solid, like a wall.

"We ought to be able to hear the freeway here, at least a little. It's not that far away."

It was then that Martha noticed how the shadows of the ruined walls reached in jagged black fingers almost to where they were sitting. It was getting very late. "It's getting awfully late," she said. "Maybe we ought to—"

"Shhh!" Ivy said. "I'm listening."

Martha listened too, until she began to feel she couldn't stand it a moment longer. Then she got up and began to wander around. At the edge of the dead garden she sat down on an old stone bench and looked back. Josie was running from place to place, stopping now and then to talk as if someone were standing right beside her—but that was something Josie often did. Ivy was still sitting very still, with her face turned toward the burned house.

Martha was beginning to feel a little desperate about getting away, when suddenly her foot, scuffling in the dirt in front of the bench, turned up something that had been lying buried in the soft dark soil. When she wiped it off, she found it was an amber-colored translucent stone, shaped in an almost perfect oval.

"Look! Look!" she screamed. "I've found the Golden Eye."

A few minutes later as Martha and Ivy were boosting Josie back over the iron fence, Ivy said, "As soon as we get the sharls stopped, we've got to come back here." She turned back up toward the house, invisible now behind the trees, and said it again. "We're going to come back."

And Martha admitted to herself that they probably would.

13

MARTHA HAD LEFT THE RUINED HOUSE THAT FIRST DAY
not at all sure she ever wanted to go back. What she
didn't at all suspect was that she herself would be the
first one to urge that they return.

It happened because Martha's mother had made
plans to take both her daughters to the city to an
afternoon performance of the ballet. Cath, who was a
Sophomore in high school that year, was still taking
ballet; but she was beginning to complain that the
lessons were taking up too much of her time. And it
turned out that that particular Saturday afternoon she
had no time at all. Pretty much at the last moment
she told her mother that there just wasn't any way
that she could fit the matinee into her schedule. And
so Mrs. Abbott asked Martha if she would like to

bring a friend. Mrs. Abbott suggested that since Kelly Peters was also a ballet student, she might be delighted to see the performance. Martha was pretty sure that Kelly wouldn't be delighted to go anywhere with her, but at her mother's insistence she called to find out. Kelly's mother answered, and she must have stayed within earshot because Kelly was ickily polite.

"Well, thanks a lot, Martha," she said. "It sure is nice of you to ask me, and I'd just love to, but today is the day that Janine is having her big roller skating party, and I already said I'd go to that. Da-a-rn!" she drawled with exaggerated regret, and the word *phony* leaped into Martha's throat in such solid form that it almost choked her. But, like always, she didn't say it.

Then Mrs. Peters must have left the room because Kelly's voice crisped, and she said, "I thought you knew about Janine's party. Nearly everybody is going."

So Martha reported to her mother that Kelly had another date and suggested, not too hopefully, that maybe Ivy could go. Somewhat to Martha's surprise, Mrs. Abbott agreed.

Martha had known that Ivy would want to go, but she was really surprised by the extent of Ivy's enthusiasm. She arrived early, combed and dressed so carefully that she hardly seemed like Ivy for a moment. On the way into the city Ivy told Martha and her mother that she had never seen a real ballet before —and not even very much on television. Aunt Evaline had no T.V., and the Carsons' set was always either broken, or being used by someone else.

"But I know a lot about it," Ivy told Mrs. Abbott. "I took lessons the last time I was in Harley's Crossing from a friend of my aunt's. And I've read books about it—and I know in other ways, too." When she said the part about "other ways," she looked at Martha and grinned. Martha grinned back, knowing that Ivy meant about having been a ballet dancer in another reincarnation.

Ordinarily, Ivy probably wouldn't have bothered to leave out something just because it might sound too unusual for an adult. Martha had heard her say some pretty fantastic things, even in front of teachers. But that day Ivy was on her most careful behavior, at least until the ballet started. From the moment that the first dancer leaped on stage, Ivy forgot about proper behavior and everything else.

Not that she did or said anything shocking, it was just that she stopped doing or saying anything at all. She just sat in her dusty red plush seat, pushed way back so far that her feet stuck almost straight out, and barely moved during the entire performance. In fact, she hardly seemed to breathe. During the intermission she managed to say, "It's wonderful," when Mrs. Abbott pressed her for a comment, but then she sank back into silence. She stayed that way all the way home.

As soon as they got home, Mrs. Abbott had to leave again to pick up Cath from where she was decorating for a dance at the high school, so Martha walked with Ivy as far as Bent Oaks. When they were almost to the grove, Ivy began to run. Martha ran after her, and when she caught up Ivy was sitting flat on the ground in the middle of the grove in her only good dress—taking off her shoes. Then she tucked her skirt up inside the legs of her underpants and began to dance.

Martha had seen Ivy dance many times before. She was always making up dances for a ceremony or ritual, and Martha had always loved watching her. Ivy danced with a wonderful kind of unity—as if no part of her existed outside of the dance—no part of her stood back to wonder how she looked. But this time the dancing was not as much fun to watch. This time, instead of just dancing, Ivy was trying to do some of the things she had just seen the ballet dancers doing. And, of course, she couldn't.

She kept trying things over and over, sometimes stopping to clench her fists or stomp her foot. Finally she came over to where Martha was sitting and dropped down beside her. Her face was flushed, and her voice sounded almost as if she were about to cry.

"It was so beautiful," she said. "And I was so sure that I could do it. I could just feel how in my arms and legs. I could feel just exactly how it would be to do such perfect—*perfect*—things, so easily and—"

"But you do beautiful things," Martha said. "The way you dance is beautiful."

"But it's not right," Ivy said. "It's not anything. I can't do the things they can do." She looked at Martha as if she were very angry. "But I'm going to, though. I'm going to learn how."

For the next few weeks it was almost as if Ivy had gone away again. Actually she was right there at Bent Oaks Grove every spare minute; but she wasn't much fun to be with. All she wanted to do was practice her dancing or read the books about ballet that she had checked out of the library. Martha and Josie waited patiently for a while, and now and then Martha even tried out a few steps herself, but after a week or two she began to get rather violently bored.

It occurred to Martha to ask Cath if it were possible for a person to teach herself to be a ballet dancer, and Cath said it wasn't. In fact, she said, most teachers didn't even like students to do much home practice between lessons because they would probably teach themselves bad habits. Martha relayed that information to Ivy, but it didn't stop her.

Ivy just nodded and said, "But that's right at first, and this isn't right at first for me. I had those lessons in Harley's Crossing, you know. And besides I remember a lot from when I was a dancer before. Not in my head, so much, but my arms and legs remember, and they're remembering more all the time."

Martha sighed and then asked resignedly, "Couldn't you take some lessons, then? Cath's teacher is supposed to be a very good one."

"No," Ivy said. "It costs too much."

"Well then, I guess you'll have to go on teaching yourself, but anyway, don't you think we could do something else for a change? We never did finish about the sharls."

"Yes," Josie said. "Let's do about the sharls."

Ivy agreed and said that maybe they could do the Tree People again the next day, but when the next day came she still wanted to dance. That was the day Martha, in desperation, started talking about the burned-out house. She remembered very well how it had made her feel, but she also remembered how intrigued Ivy had seemed by it—and it was a time for extreme measures. She talked about the strangeness of the place and the sad silence, and finally she saw that Ivy was really beginning to listen. The next day they went back to the burned-out house.

As soon as they were back beneath the black edged walls, Martha wished they hadn't come. Somehow it seemed worse than before. Maybe it was the weather, cold and gray and threatening, that made the sadness of the place seem bitterer and less intriguing. Even Ivy seemed a little uneasy at first.

But they had come to explore and so they did. They poked around for a while in a dry fishpond and grotto fashioned out of large rough rocks and agreed that if it were only closer to home it would be a wonderful place for the Lower Level. Then in what seemed to have been a kind of kitchen garden, they discovered a weathered trash heap, that when prodded by sharp sticks yielded old purpling bottles and a rusty dinner fork. Not far from the trash heap there was a stone bench, and Martha and Ivy sat down on it facing the house while Josie wandered around digging little holes with the bent fork.

Staring up at the ruin, Martha imagined what it must have looked like once. A tall old-fashioned house with fancy carved trim and two or maybe three stories of high thin windows. Then without planning to, she started imagining it another way, with thin tongues of flame licking out of all the windows and springing up through the roof in huge red hands against the sky.

Suddenly Ivy asked, "Do you know the story of what happened here?"

"No," Martha said. "I asked my mother about it, and she said it happened a long time ago. She said she'd heard something about it, but she couldn't remember just what. Except that the same people own it who own the land around Bent Oaks. There's an old man who won't let anything be sold or changed."

Ivy was quiet again for a while longer, and then she said, "Well, I know about it now. It belonged to a beautiful lady named Annabelle and her husband. It was a long time ago, and they were very rich. Annabelle had been the most beautiful girl for miles and miles, and she married a very handsome man and he built this house for her and gave her all sorts of beautiful jewels and clothes and servants and everything she asked for. After a few years they had three beauti-ful children. But Annabelle wasn't happy because she was used to going to dances and parties all the time, and now she had to stay home with the babies while her husband went away to work. One day there was going to be a very important party at the king's palace—"

"The *king's* palace?" Martha said. "Here, in Rose-wood Hills?"

"Well, maybe it was at the mayor's house. Any-way, Annabelle wanted to go, but her husband had to go away on business, and he said she shouldn't go without him."

Martha interrupted again, "Who told you? Did your mother know about it?"

"No," Ivy said. "My mother didn't tell me. I think I heard about it somewhere a long time ago and I just started remembering. It just sort of came to me. Don't things just sort of come to you sometimes?"

Martha considered. "Yes, I guess they do. I think it just came to me what happened next—to Annabelle, I mean."

"What?" Ivy said.

"Well, Annabelle went off to the party without telling anyone, and in the night the fire started and —" she stopped, not quite sure she wanted to end it the way she was thinking.

"—and then Annabelle came back and the chil-dren were all dead, and the next day her hair turned

125

snow white, and the next day she died."

Martha nodded slowly, and they went on sitting there staring at the ruin for a long time. They came back, finally, through time and tragedy, to the sound of Josie's chatter and the realization that the gray cold had reached almost to the center of their bones.

Martha turned to Ivy, and they both said, "Let's go home," in perfect unison.

But this time Josie didn't want to go. She sat firmly on the ground with her chubby legs out in front of her, clutching the old fork and a bouquet of dead flowers. She scowled at them and refused to stand up. At last Ivy took the flowers and fork by force, and, grabbing her hands, Martha and Ivy pulled Josie to her feet and started down the hill. Josie wailed and struggled.

"I want my pretty flowers," Josie sobbed.

Ivy sighed and looked back up the hill. "What do you want those old dead things for?" she asked.

"They're not your flowers," Martha said, trying another tack. "They don't belong to us."

"Yes they do, yes they do," Josie said.

"They belong here, to this house. They belong to a beautiful dead lady."

"No they don't," Josie said. "They belong to me. The lady gave them to me."

Martha looked at Ivy, and Ivy's nod meant that she was wondering the same thing.

"What lady, Josie?" Ivy asked.

"The lady you said," Josie said. "The beautiful dead lady."

"How do you know she was a dead lady?" Martha asked in a stiff voice that tightened into a gulp before she finished the sentence.

"She said she was," Josie said. "She said she was the beautiful dead lady."

"Did she have white hair?" Ivy asked.

Josie thought a minute and then nodded. "White," she said, putting her hand on top of her head.

"What else did she say to you?"

"She said she was the beautiful dead lady, and I could have some flowers," Josie said.

So Martha and Ivy went, very quickly and watchfully, back up the hill for the flowers; and then, all the way home, while Josie trudged happily along carrying the little dead bouquet, they walked just behind her, watching and wondering.

14

FOR THE NEXT FEW DAYS MARTHA AND IVY TALKED A lot about the burned-out house and what had happened there, and for the next few days after that, they talked about going back. But before they got to the point of actually going, something else happened. Martha's Grandmother Abbott sent money from Florida for all the Abbotts to fly down and spend Thanksgiving with her.

Of course it occurred to Martha that the whole controversy about her staying for a while with Grandmother in Florida might be renewed if she actually was there, right in Grandmother's clutches. It was certainly a very great danger. And it had all happened so quickly that there was only one afternoon to discuss it with Ivy. She moaned to Ivy about her fear that she might have to stay.

"Well, don't just sit there," Ivy said. "Let's do a spell again."

"Again?" Martha said. "How?"

"With Josie. She saved you before."

"I know but—she can't give me the mumps again. I've already had them—on both sides."

"I know. It wouldn't be the same anyway, even if you could get mumps twice. Magic doesn't do things the way you expect. If it did, it wouldn't be magic."

"I guess not. How do we do it this time?"

"Well, I'll go home and get Josie. And you fix up the altar." She called the last back over her shoulder as she started to run toward the trail.

"But how?" Martha called. "Wait. I don't know how."

Ivy stopped, but she didn't come back. "You don't need to know how. Just start doing it. You find out as you go along."

When Ivy came back towing an out of breath Josie, Martha had made up an altar on the flat rock near Temple Tree. She had draped the rock first with the Mousehole Quilt, and then she had placed four sacred objects around the edges at the four points of the compass. There was the Crystal Globe to the South, the Golden Eye to the North, and East and West, Josie's ivory wand and the silver bell.

"Very good," Ivy said when she saw the altar. She lifted Josie up and made her sit cross-legged in the center of the magic circle. Josie grinned happily. She loved ceremonies.

Ivy began by ringing the silver bell. Then Martha rang it, and finally Josie. While Josie went on ringing it long and hard, Ivy said, "We'll need a chant. Let's sit down like this and see if a good one will come to us. Keep on ringing the bell, Josie." They sat down cross-legged and covered their eyes with their hands.

After a moment Martha said, "Maker of spells, hear our silver bell."

Ivy nodded and shortly after added, "Ring a magic chain, to pull Martha home again."

The chant was repeated over and over while Martha and Ivy walked backward around Josie and the altar. Next they breathed on the Golden Eye and held it to their hearts while they waved the magic wand. Finally they put the Golden Eye in one of Josie's hands and the ivory wand in the other, and placed the Crystal Globe directly in front of her. "Now you look into the Globe while we sit here, and when you see that the spell is finished you can tell us."

"Okay," Josie said. Martha and Ivy sat down in front of the altar and covered their eyes, and in a very short time Josie said, "All finished."

They looked up and Martha said, "Did the magic work? Is the spell going to work? Can you tell?"

She was really talking to Ivy, but Josie answered. She leaned forward until her nose almost touched the Globe and said, "Yes," very definitely.

"Will Martha have to stay in Florida?" Ivy asked.

"No," Josie said.

"How come?" Martha said. "Why won't I have to stay?"

Josie leaned forward again and then sat up looking triumphant.

"Your mommy won't let you," she said.

Martha and Ivy had to giggle. It didn't sound like a very magical reason. And it didn't seem very likely, either. Martha's mother had been all for the plan to send Martha away. It wouldn't be like her to change her mind so completely.

So the Abbotts flew off to Florida, and almost right away Josie's magic started working; although Martha didn't realize at first that that was what it was. She didn't blame herself very much, though. Nobody would recognize magic in two-toned shoes and a pin-striped suit.

The first thing Martha did notice that told her the magic was working was that her mother certainly was changing her mind. Suddenly she not only didn't want Martha to stay in Florida, she didn't even want Grandmother Abbott to stay. Usually Mrs. Abbott was not at all upset by her mother-in-law's frequent visits to Florida, or to anyplace else. But this year she decided that that Grandmother just had to be in Rosewood for the holiday season. And Martha's father seemed to agree. In fact they agreed so unusually well that they finally talked Grandmother into closing her apartment and coming back with them to Rosewood Hills.

Ivy had explained that magic worked in unexpected ways and she was certainly right. This time it was so unexpected that Martha might never have known just what was happening if she hadn't overheard a conversation between Tom and Cath. The three of them were lying on the beach, and Martha was pretending to be asleep, with her face under a big sun hat.

"How come Mom keeps fussing at Gran to come home with us?" Tom asked idly as if he didn't really expect an answer. But Cath knew why. You could always count on Cath to know a lot about almost anything you'd care to mention.

"You mean you don't know?" Cath sounded incredulous that anyone could be so dense. "It's because of that Mr. Millmore. He's always hanging around, and Mother says he's planning to marry Grandmother."

Martha was amazed. Mr. Millmore was a young-old man with wavy silver hair and pin-striped suits who happened to be a neighbor of Grandmother's in her new apartment. He had called on her two or three times while the rest of the Abbotts were there, and he was very helpful and friendly. But Martha had certainly not guessed that he was part of the magic.

Seen through the cracks in her straw sun hat, Tom looked as astounded as Martha felt.

"Marry her," he said, and then after a silence,

"Did he ask her or something?"

"Not that Mom knows of," Cath said. "But she can tell that he's going to as soon as we're out of the way."

"Oh yeah?" Tom said. "What do you know." But then in a minute he laughed. "Well, why not let him?" he said. "He may not be great, but he's bound to be better than all those garden clubs."

Cath snorted. "Idiot," she said. "What about the inheritance?"

Tom sobered. "Oh yeah," he said. "I see what you mean."

All the Abbotts knew about the inheritance. It was a large and powerful sum of money that Grandfather Abbott had left to Grandmother Abbott when he died. It was supposed to be left to the rest of the Abbotts someday. But not, of course, if it was left to somebody else.

Martha had thought that Mr. Millmore was rather nice, and she couldn't help thinking that Tom was probably right about his being better than garden clubs. She'd been to a few with Grandmother, and she had reason to know. However, she also felt that she should just accept Mr. Millmore as a part of Josie's magic and be glad that he had made it necessary for *all* the Abbotts to return to Rosewood Hills.

So Martha went back to Rosewood Manor Estates, number two Castle Court, where everybody seemed to go right on getting busier and busier according to mysteriously complicated and demanding sets of rules and patterns. All except Martha, of course, who never seemed to be able to find a set of rules that worked for her.

But she also went back to Bent Oaks Grove, where it didn't matter if you didn't know the rules because you could always make them up as you went along.

And then, only a few days after Christmas, the Carson family packed up and left with no warning, and Ivy was gone again.

15

IT WAS ANOTHER LONG AND LONELY TIME IN MARTHA'S life. She finished the sixth grade and went into the seventh with very mixed-up feelings about almost everything. She was happier, at times, and at others a lot more unhappy than she had ever been before. Everything stayed disgustingly the same—and at the same time changed so rapidly that she sometimes felt there was nothing she could count on as being finally true.

Everything about number two Castle Court was the same, and the people in it were, too, except that Cath became a Junior in high school and Tom a Sophomore and their friends were very grown-up—at least in some ways. Cath's friends wore crazy beautiful clothes and treated everybody and everything as if they were a part of some huge ridiculous joke. They laughed a lot, very loudly. Tom's friends were mostly huge football types with crew cuts, and they were even noisier than Cath's friends, without trying half so hard.

Martha did a lot of watching, and sometimes it all seemed very exciting. And there were times when she almost felt a part of it. Sometimes Cath's friends included her in their conversation without talking to her as if she were a retarded five-year-old; and once one of Tom's friends, a very important fullback on the high school team, grabbed her by the hair. She was on her way to the back door at the time, and she had to squeeze through the kitchen, which was practically wall to wall with boys, particularly near the refrigerator. As she squeezed past the fullback, whose name was Grant Wilson, he reached out and grabbed her long hair and held it way up above her head so she couldn't move.

"Hey, look what I caught," he yelled, and they all looked around. Then he yelled at Tom, "Is this that homely little sister you used to have? Well, what do you know. She may not turn out so bad, after all." Martha nearly died of embarrassment, but afterwards she thought about very little else for several days.

Another amazing change, that turned out not to be a real change, was the behavior of Kelly Peters. Towards the end of the seventh grade, Kelly suddenly became very friendly with Martha—at least at times. The times were usually when Martha was at home, and after a while Martha began to realize that Kelly nearly always felt friendliest when Tom was around. Gradually it became obvious that Kelly was crazy about Tom Abbott, who was three years older than she was and naturally thought of her as a little kid.

But even after Martha knew for certain the reason behind Kelly's sudden change of heart, she sometimes had a hard time keeping it in mind. Kelly and two or three of her close friends were the absolute rulers of seventh grade society. Everybody followed their lead in just about everything, and Martha certainly wasn't cut out to be any kind of a counter force. So sometimes when she was asked, she made the effort and worked very hard at talking about the right things in the right tone of voice, at squealing with laughter at the right times and at cutting down the right people with the right kind of sarcasm.

But afterwards, or sometimes even in the middle of things, she would suddenly be overcome with a terrible feeling that it was all phony and unreal. She was never positive if the worst of the phoniness was her own or everybody else's; but whichever, it would suddenly seem just too much of an effort and she would turn quiet and strange and escape to her room and her books, and sometimes to Bent Oaks Grove.

At Bent Oaks she often climbed up to Falcon's Roost or to the Lookout. Sometimes she took a book along, but at other times she just sat there for a while with her thoughts and memories, often about Ivy.

Thinking about Ivy was almost always good. Sometimes Martha wondered and even worried a little about what Ivy was doing and what it would be like when she came back. But usually it seemed to Martha that nothing, not a single event in her present life, compared to the adventure of almost every day when Ivy was around.

But no matter what else she was thinking, there was one thing Martha never doubted. She never doubted that Ivy would be back. In fact, the feeling that Ivy might show up at any moment was so strong that Martha often found herself looking for Ivy, particularly when she was in Bent Oaks Grove. When she was in the grove, she was constantly looking up along the trail, expecting to see Ivy appear over the top of the hill. But no one ever came.

At least, no one came until a few weeks after school started, the fall Martha was in the eighth grade. It was a very hot end-of-summer day, and after school Martha put on some shorts and picked out a book to read. Then she climbed up to Bent Oaks Grove where the coolness of the ocean breeze almost always flowed over the top of Rosewood Hills and spilled through the branches of the oak trees. There were some little kids at Bent Oaks that day who were playing in the best reading spot in Falcon's Roost, so Martha climbed higher. She settled herself in the wide fork that had been called the Lookout, and began to read. She hadn't been reading very long when something made her look up toward the place where the trail looped over the top of the hill. Just at that moment someone was coming into view over the crest. Someone small and dark, who stopped at the top of the hill, looked all around, and then started to run down the trail. Plunging headlong down the steep trail, the figure skipped around the zigzag turns as lightly as if there were no such things as gravity and slippery pebbles. It had to be Ivy. Martha stood up carelessly on a narrow branch, and hanging on with just one hand she waved the other arm wildly and screamed, "Ivy!"

The force of the yell surprised Martha, herself, and must have scared the kids playing in Falcon's Roost half to death. Martha yelled again, and down below her the little kids sat staring upwards with their mouths hanging open. Up on the trail Ivy stopped almost in mid-jump to listen. Martha waved again, and then Ivy waved back and began to run faster than ever. In only a minute she was in the grove and swarming up the trunk of Tower Tree, right through Falcon's Roost and the staring kids, and on up the harder climb to the Lookout.

When Ivy had pulled herself up the last few feet to the Lookout, Martha scooted over to make room, and for a minute they just sat staring at each other and laughing.

"Hi," Ivy said, and the word came out halfway between a gasp for air and a giggle.

"Hi," Martha said back.

Then they sat for another minute before Martha said, "I knew you were coming. I had a feeling and I just looked up and there you were."

"I know," Ivy said. "I knew you'd be here in the grove, too. Do you still come here a lot? Since I've been gone, I mean?"

"Sometimes," Martha said. "Not nearly as much as I used to. As we used to, I mean."

Ivy nodded and looked down around the grove. "We sure used to come here a lot," she said. "It looks just the same as always."

It seemed safest to talk first about the grove and the past and all the things they used to do together, and next they talked about the more recent past and the things they had been doing since Ivy went away. Martha told what there was to tell about the Abbotts, and what it was like at school; and Ivy talked sparingly about where she had been in the almost two years she had been away.

The Carsons had spent almost a year in Texas, and from there they had moved to an apartment house in Chicago. There had been two months in the summer when Ivy had gone back to Harley's Crossing to live with her Aunt Evaline. Aunt Evaline had felt well enough in the summer to go home to Harley's Crossing, and she had sent for Ivy. It had been a wonderful two months. Two wonderful free green months after the gray closed-in-ness of Chicago. They had lived outdoors most of the time, and the woods were beautiful. But then Aunt Evaline had to go back to the rest home, and Ivy went back to Chicago.

"Chicago?" Martha asked. "What were you doing there? Did your father have a job there?"

Ivy shrugged. "Something like that. It had something to do with trucks. A guy he met in Texas had something to do with it. There were a lot of trucks, and they were shipping things different places."

"They?" Martha asked.

"My father and my brothers—Max and Randy. I never heard much about it. But after a while Max disappeared, and I guess he went to jail; so what ever they were doing must have had something fishy about it. They never talked about it, or about where Max went, while I was around; but I doubt if he went on a vacation to Florida." Ivy stopped and waited for Martha to comment, and Martha saw that it was a kind of test.

So Martha said unconcernedly, "What was it like —living in a big city?" The way she said it meant that it didn't matter about Max. She had understood what Ivy was asking, and Ivy understood Martha, too. There was nothing new about that. Understanding each other without words was the way it had always been. But Martha felt right way that something was different. The difference was how much it really *did* matter about Max—to Ivy.

"It was horrible," Ivy said. "We lived in an apart-

142

ment building on the ninth floor."

"The ninth floor!" Martha said. It was hard to imagine Ivy living like that, with no place to get away to. "I just can't imagine you on the ninth floor."

"Neither could I. I was about to leave when all of a sudden we came back here."

"You were about to leave," Martha asked. "You mean all by yourself?"

"Yes, or maybe with Josie. I was going to take her with me. I was planning to run away."

"Ivy!" Martha gasped. She could see it all too clearly—Ivy with no one except Josie, with a bundle on a stick, alone in a dark canyon of a city street, where strange figures lurked in doorways and the mouths of narrow alleys brimmed with horrors.

"Well, I was going to," Ivy said as fiercely as if Martha had really argued about it. "I almost did. But I didn't have to because, just in time, we packed up and left. So now the Carsons are back again on the wrong side of Rosewood Hills, and here I am."

"Do you think you'll stay? Very long, I mean?" Martha asked.

"I don't know. I think we left last time because my father owed somebody a lot of money. I don't suppose he's paid it. He never does."

Martha was beginning to feel really shocked and frightened. Not by what Ivy said about owing money, although being in debt *was* an important sin in the Abbotts' catechism. It wasn't any of the things Ivy said about her family—because Martha had always known those things, and worse, about the Carsons. It had more to do with the way Ivy talked about them. Always before, when Ivy talked about the Carsons, it was with a coolness, a kind of distance. It had been almost the same way she talked about the people of the Land of the Green Sky, or Annabelle of the burned-out-house. But now the distance was gone, and Ivy's face was tight and hot; and suddenly the Carsons seemed much more close and real—and Ivy much more a part of them.

A question leaped into Martha's mind. "Hey," she said, "remember how you used to say you were a changeling? Are you still a changeling?"

Ivy laughed, stuck out her lower lip and blew upward to untangle a curly wisp of hair from her long eyelashes, exactly the way she always had. "Sure," she said. "You're either a changeling or you aren't." She grinned wickedly. "Any day now I'm going to fly off on a broom—or maybe I'll start sprouting horns and a tail and turn into a monster."

"You don't show any signs of it yet," Martha said. "You look just about the same as you always have."

Ivy looked at Martha with her head on one side. "Well, you don't. You've changed." It sounded like an accusation, and Martha suddenly felt guilty.

Martha looked down at herself uneasily. She was much slimmer in most places, and quite a bit taller; and except for the retainer, the braces were finally gone from her teeth.

"Everyone says I look better," she said.

"You look pretty," Ivy said, matter of factly, as if it hardly mattered. "But you're starting to look grown-up already. Look at that." She pointed to the front of Martha's Tee-shirt.

"Oh that," Martha hunched her shoulders and grinned sheepishly. "That's mostly the bra I'm wearing. I borrowed it from Cath."

"Oh," Ivy said. It was a perfectly blank-faced "Oh," but Martha heard all sorts of questions and judgments in it.

"Well," she said defensively, "all the other girls wear them."

Ivy only looked thoughtful, but after a minute she said almost fiercely, "I am *never* going to grow up."

"How can you help it?"

"I can. I'll just refuse to. You could too if you wanted to."

"You mean you think we can really stop growing?"

"No. We'll go on growing in some ways I guess. That's not what counts. Aunt Evaline says that lots and lots of people never grow up. But there are good ways and bad ways to do it."

"What's the difference?"

"I'm not too sure yet. But it has something to do with knowing what you're doing, I guess. It's the ones who think they are grown up and aren't who are really messed up."

"And what's it like if you do it the right way?"

"Well, it's like—Aunt Evaline, for instance. And you know who else? Mrs. Smith."

"Mrs. Smith?"

"Sure. There are all sorts of ways you can tell about Mrs. Smith."

"Well, she looks pretty old to me."

"Oh, you mean her hair's gray and like that. Well sure, but that's not what counts. What counts is the way she does things. Don't you remember how she always does everything almost like it's a game. And the way she is with animals. Even the way she walks."

"The way she walks?"

"Umm," Ivy said. "She kind of skips. Even if she doesn't really, she always seems about to."

"Oh yes," Martha said. "I know what you mean. About Mrs. Smith anyway. But how do you do it? How could *we* do it?"

"I'm not sure yet, but I've been working on it. One thing, I know it won't be easy because we've waited too long. We're really too old already. Eleven would have been the best time. Eleven is just about the best age for almost everything."

"Well, I guess we're too late for that," Martha said.

"Maybe, unless we can go backward. It might be possible. I'm going to think about it."

16

The day after Ivy came back, Martha and Ivy met early to go over the old Ridge Trail to the Onowora Stables to see Mrs. Smith. On the way Ivy talked again about the problem of being too old.

"I've been thinking about it," Ivy said, "and I really believe we ought to do something about it. I mean, there must be some way to keep from letting yourself just go on and on until you wake up someday and find out you've turned into an ordinary adult."

Martha didn't know quite what to say. For one thing, she wasn't absolutely sure that Ivy was serious. She seemed to be, but Martha felt a little uncertain. Ivy had been gone such a long time, Martha felt it was possible that she was out of practice in understanding just what Ivy meant by the strange things she sometimes said. As they walked, Martha watched Ivy carefully for clues.

They were walking single file along the narrow trail. Ivy was walking ahead, looking back over her shoulder now and then as she talked. She was wearing a very childish dress for an eighth grader—a cotton dress with gathered fullness in rows of faded smocking across the chest. Her feet were bare and dusty, and her hair, in its one thick braid, hung far below her waist. Her small thin face seemed more overpowered than ever by her amazing eyes. Ivy's eyes had always seemed almost supernatural, but now there seemed to be even more of a difference about them, and Martha was beginning to feel more and more that there was a deep and hidden difference about Ivy, herself. Sometimes it wasn't there at all, but it flickered up now and then like a flame, burning and angry.

Halfway along Martha asked, "What's wrong with being an adult?" and without warning, the flame flared.

"If you don't know, there's no use trying to tell you."

They walked on, silently. Martha wanted to say something, but she didn't know what. Besides, she could tell it wouldn't do any good as long as Ivy held her head stiff and kicked at the dust with her bare feet. But then suddenly, there was a lizard lying in the trail and Ivy squatted down beside it. Martha went down beside her, and they waited silently for the lizard to move.

"Do you think it's dead?" Martha asked.

Ivy glanced up and her eyes were cool again, but clouded with worry. "I don't think so. He moved a little as we came up. He's hurt, though."

"Part of his tail is gone," Martha said. "Something must have tried to catch him, and his tail came off as he got away."

Ivy nodded. "Maybe he's just not over the shock," she said. She touched him with her finger tip. "He's very cold. Maybe some sun would help."

"Lizards like the sun," Martha agreed.

Ivy picked the lizard up gently and carried him to a sunny rock. "There," she said. "Do you feel any better?" The lizard raised his head and looked at them, and Martha and Ivy looked at each other and smiled.

"I've been thinking about it," Martha said as they started on, "and I think you're right about eleven being the best age of all." It was the truth, too. She *had* been thinking about it—about how nice things had been when they were eleven—how simple it was then to have a private world like Bent Oaks Grove, and how much easier it was to keep your various worlds apart when you needed to.

Ivy flicked a grin back at Martha and ran and jumped up onto a dead log.

"About what's wrong with grown-ups," she said, balancing along the log like a tightrope walker, "is that they think they know all the answers."

"I know," Martha said, nodding hard. "They really do."

"No they don't," Ivy said. "It would be impossible." She tried to walk out on a narrow branch leading from the main trunk of the dead tree. "Immmm-possible," she said again as she fell off.

Martha laughed. "That's what I meant," she said. "That they really do *think* they know all the answers. They think it's terribly important to know all the answers."

"Oh," Ivy said. She got up off the ground and got back on the trunk of the tree. She started off on the branch again holding her arms out for balance. "The answers aren't important really," she said. "What's important is—is—is—" she stopped because she had reached a very narrow bouncy part and was balancing along it toward where it almost touched a big boulder. She wavered, caught herself, and riding the bounce she jumped from the branch to the boulder. "What's important is," she went on as she scrambled up the side of the rock, "what's important is—" She reached the top and threw up her arms in a gesture of victory. Then she grinned down at Martha with her hands on her hips, "What's important is—knowing all the questions." She collapsed then on top of the rock giggling, and Martha scrambled up beside her. They sat there giggling on top of the rock for quite a while, leaning against each other's backs.

When they were finally walking along the trail

again, Ivy said, "I think that's part of it, all right."

"Of what?"

"Part of the spell. I've been trying to think up a good spell to say to enchant us into never growing up. And that's going to be part of it. That about knowing the questions."

"Know all the questions, but not the answers," Martha chanted. "Like that?"

"Yes," Ivy said. "Just like that. Remember the spell we did to keep you from staying in Florida?"

"Well, not exactly every word of it. But I remember some of the words. And I remember how it worked! Mr. Millmore. And I remember how you said that was the way with magic—that it never does the thing you expect, that magic is never the same twice."

"Hey, that's some more of it," Ivy said. "Always different—and never the same." Ivy stopped and breathed deeply. "We're almost there," she said. "I can smell the stables."

Martha sniffed. "Me too. Doesn't it smell great? I think the smell of horses is the most exciting smell in the world. Don't you?"

"Ummhuh," Ivy said and started to run. They ran the rest of the way down the path to the back fence, and scrambling over it, they went on running, clear to the door of the stables. From there they went very slowly, saying hello to all the old horses with pats and scratches, and introducing Ivy to the new ones that had come since she went away. After the horses, they went looking for Mrs. Smith at the house.

It turned out that Mrs. Smith was painting somewhere near the lake, so Martha and Ivy decided to look for her there. They were part way through the north pasture when they saw Mrs. Smith standing in front of her easel, far down toward the lake. They ran to the fence, climbed up on it and yelled and waved. As soon as she saw them, Mrs. Smith waved back and started running toward them.

Ivy looked at Martha significantly. "See what I mean about her?" she said. "Real ordinary adults just don't run like that."

And when Mrs. Smith reached them, she hugged them both at once, without even stopping to wipe her painty hands.

The three of them walked down to the easel to see what Mrs. Smith was doing. "What do you think of it?" she asked.

"Is that an old man or a tree?" Martha asked. Mrs. Smith didn't answer, so she added, "Or both?"

"Or the ghost of both?" Ivy said.

"Or the ghost of winter?" Martha said.

Mrs. Smith laughed. "I was beginning to wonder, myself," she said. "Thanks for helping me decide. Have an orange. There's some in the basket."

So they climbed up on the fence and sat eating oranges which smelled just slightly of turpentine, and talked about what they had been doing. That is, Martha and Mrs. Smith did. Ivy said very little, and

Martha guessed that she didn't want to talk about the Carsons, even to Mrs. Smith. Finally Mrs. Smith asked Ivy a direct question.

"And what have you been doing since you left Rosewood Hills?"

Ivy shrugged, "Nothing. Nothing much. Waiting mostly. Just waiting."

"Waiting?" Mrs. Smith asked, but Ivy didn't answer, so Mrs. Smith answered for her. "For the future, I guess? What are you planning for the future, Ivy? What are you planning to do when you're grown-up?"

Martha started to smile, and then Ivy did, too.

"Did I say something funny?" Mrs. Smith asked.

"It's just that Ivy is never going to grow up. We've just been talking about it. Ivy is making a spell so that she will never have to grow up."

"Wonderful," Mrs. Smith said. "I want to hear about that, too. But first I want you to tell me what you are planning to be doing when you are *not* grown-up, about ten years from now."

Ivy nodded. "Okay. I'll be a great ballet dancer. I'm going to study in a school in New York, and then I'm going to dance all over the world."

"She's already studied some with a lady in Harley's Crossing who's a friend of her aunt's," Martha said.

So then Ivy told Mrs. Smith about Mrs. W. who had been a great dancer herself once, and who had some friends in New York that Ivy could live with and study ballet, some day when she was older and had some money for the school.

"And what are you going to be?" Mrs. Smith asked Martha.

Martha was thinking about an answer when Ivy said, "Martha is going to be a famous star of stage and screen."

"I am?" Martha began to giggle. "It's the first I've heard about it."

But Mrs. Smith didn't seem to see that it was a joke. "Yes," she said, "I wouldn't be surprised. And what is this about not growing up?"

"Well," Ivy was grinning wickedly, "we were talking about people who never grew up, and we decided you were one."

Mrs. Smith laughed. "So that's what's the matter with me. I've always wondered."

"No really," Ivy said. "We were talking about people who never turn into 'Grown-Ups.'" When she said "Grown-Ups," she stuck out her chest and chin and looked down her nose. "You know. That kind."

"Yes," Mrs. Smith said. "I think I know exactly what you mean."

When Mrs. Smith had to go home to make lunch, Martha and Ivy started home. On the way, they began working on the spell again. They worked back and forth, suggesting lines and improving on them until they were satisfied. Then they started running, chanting the lines over and over as they ran. The chant went—"Know all the Questions, but not the Answers

—Look for the Different, instead of the Same—Never Walk where there's room for Running—Don't do anything that can't be a Game."

As they went they chanted louder and louder and ran wilder and wilder, scrambling up rocks and jumping off, jumping up to swing on tree branches and rolling down grassy slopes. When they reached Bent Oaks Grove, they ran, staggering a little from exhaustion, right through the Entry Gates and across the grove to Tower Tree. Two little girls playing house in the cave stopped, frozen with amazement, as Martha and Ivy staggered and chanted across the grove and up the tree as far as Falcon's Roost.

In the Roost, they collapsed, laughing and gasping for breath. It took quite a while for the laughing and gasping to die down enough to let them speak. Then they peeked out of the roost and started laughing all over again when they caught sight of the little girls tiptoeing out of the grove carrying their dolls and playhouse stuff.

"They probably think we just escaped from the insane asylum," Martha gasped. "Poor things. They probably think we might get violent any minute." She pulled her hair down over her face and pretended to come at Ivy with claws and fangs. Ivy pretended back for a minute, before they both collapsed again.

They were both quiet for several minutes before Ivy said, "You see? It really works. I feel a whole lot younger already. Don't you?"

156

17

THAT VERY NIGHT AFTER SPENDING A WHOLE DAY, A
really great day, with Ivy, Martha made a shocking
discovery. What she discovered was hard to see clearly,
and it could be looked at from different angles, but
mainly it looked a lot like treachery. She began to
recognize it as treachery while she was lying in bed
very late that night, trying to go to sleep. Instead she
kept thinking, and worrying about Monday.

Monday was the day Ivy would be starting school
again in Rosewood Hills, and this time it would be
junior high school. The junior high at Rosewood was
seventh and eighth grades, and it was on the same
grounds as the elementary school, but in a separate
wing, and things were different there. There was real
P.E. with uniforms and showers, and you had several

teachers instead of one, but those weren't the most important differences. There were other changes that mattered more.

The other times Ivy was at Rosewood, Martha and Ivy had been together almost every moment of the school day. They had met on the corner of Castle Court and walked together to school. They had spent every recess together, and whenever possible they sat next to each other in class. That was the way things had always been.

But now there were some other things to consider. There was, for instance, the fact that Martha had been walking to school with other people sometimes lately —sometimes even with Kelly and her gang of friends.

Kelly went to school every morning in the middle of a procession, or maybe it was a swarm. It was like a swarm in that it swirled around Kelly, who was, of course, the queen bee. Around Kelly were five or six of her girl friends, and around them on the fringes there were boys—usually several boys. The swarm, circling and maneuvering, moved down the steep sidewalks of Rosewood Hills announced and followed by a constant roar of laugher and loud conversation. Stragglers and smaller groups often followed along behind, but you didn't actually join Kelly's gang unless you were asked.

Several times, since the beginning of eighth grade, Kelly had started her morning parade by crossing over to the Abbott's house—and asking if Martha was ready to leave for school. At the Abbotts' house Tom usually answered the door, and Martha never was ready. So Kelly would wait sweetly and patiently, talking to Tom, while Martha feverishly combed her hair and gathered her books. Martha wasn't ready because she had long before made it a habit to wait until the last minute before leaving for school. She had developed the habit for a very particular reason—in order to avoid being passed—and passed up—by Kelly and her gang.

Being a part of Kelly's morning procession was something like being a part of a stampede—wildly exciting, but at any moment you might fall and be trampled. Martha had had a taste of the trampling. It had happened when a particular boy was paying too much attention to Martha.

Kelly had attacked with practiced skill. She twirled around Martha first, attracting everyone's attention to what she was doing. "Hey, Marty," she began sweetly. "What are all those *bi-i-g* books you're carrying? I've never seen so many *bi-i-i-g* fat books. You must be working too hard."

"No, I'm not," Martha stammered. "Most of these are just library books. This one and this one are just—"

"Oh, don't tell me about them, for heaven's sake. I'm not really that interested. I'm just not the bookworm type, I guess. I've got other things to think about." She dimpled cutely at Linda Nelson and Darlene Sutter. "Haven't you got other things to think about than big old boring books?"

Then she had skipped away leaving Martha miserably pretending she hadn't minded, and that it was all a joke—because she didn't have courage enough to do anything else.

But now there was Ivy to think about; and Martha was amazed to find that the way she felt about Ivy seemed to change from moment to moment. Of course, it was wonderful to have Ivy back—the best thing that could possibly happen—but— Thinking it over, Martha was forced to admit that the "but" was because no one, not even Martha, could imagine Ivy Carson as a part of Kelly Peters' gang.

Martha was awake for a long time that night, wondering how her feelings could go in two opposite directions at practically the same time, and just how different Monday was going to be. Finally, though, she realized that she was doing exactly what the spell she and Ivy had made up had said not to do. She was being afraid of differences.

She started saying the spell over and over to herself very softly, like counting sheep. "Know all the Questions, but not the Answers—Look for the Different instead of the Same—Never Walk where there's room for Running—Don't do anything that can't be a Game." The next thing she knew it was morning.

Martha met Ivy, just as she always had, on the corner of Castle Court, and they walked together to school. Ivy was looking the same as always, too. Wisps of curly hair escaping from her thick braid made tangled corkscrews around her face; and, of course, that year hair was supposed to swing straight and slick as straw. Ivy wore no makeup, not even eye makeup, which was being worn by almost every other girl in the eighth grade class. And Ivy's dress was the worst of all. It was the same smocked and checkered cotton that she had worn the day before.

Martha had barely had time to say hello when they turned a corner and came upon Kelly's gang, which had stopped to admire a dune buggy parked in front of the Wilsons' house. Everyone had heard that Grant Wilson was getting a dune buggy, but hardly anyone had seen it yet.

Two years before Ivy would probably have yelled hello at Kelly's gang, not caring who might yell back and who might not. But now she only grinned crookedly at Martha and walked faster, just as Martha was doing. Because they were on the other side of the street, Martha hoped that they might get by without being noticed. But suddenly Kelly said, "Hey, isn't that Ivy Carson?"

Kelly's voice was whispery in tone, but just a fraction under the very top-of-her-lungs in volume. "Hey, that *is* Ivy Carson," she said. "I thought they got chased out of the state."

As usual Kelly showed a whole lot of technique. Her whisper had been just soft enough to pretend that she hadn't meant for Ivy to overhear, and just loud enough to be absolutely sure she did.

Brad Jenkins, a tall pimply boy and one of Kelly's most adoring admirers, followed her lead. "Hey, Carson," he yelled. "Where you been? In jail?" Kelly rewarded him with a giggle and he got carried away. "What's that you're wearing, Carson? A tablecloth?"

Ivy stopped walking and stood still; and her face was hard and burning, a Carson face. Martha grabbed Ivy's arm and tried to pull her on.

"Come on, Ivy," she pleaded. "Don't pay any attention." But Ivy jerked her arm away and walked slowly across the street. Most of Kelly's gang stopped to watch her come.

She went up to Brad Jenkins first, right up until she could have touched him. She looked in his face and kept looking. Brad blinked and swallowed.

"Hi, Brad Jenkins," was all Ivy said, but Brad jumped as if something had exploded in his face. Then Ivy turned to Kelly. "Hi Kelly," she said. "You look different, but I guess you're just as mean as ever."

Surprise seemed to keep Kelly speechless for one second too long, while Ivy turned and started back across the street. Then she almost screamed after Ivy, "Who do you think you are? You crummy jailbird."

Even Martha could tell that Kelly's answer was a mistake. It was too angry, too corny, and too out-and-out honestly mean. Kelly had lost, for a moment, her usual—and much admired—cool. The points went to Ivy, and all the people who mattered most to Kelly had seen it happen. Martha knew that that meant there would be trouble, real trouble. There was no doubt about it. She hadn't lived next to Kelly Peters all her life for nothing.

But the trouble was slower in coming than Martha expected. Days passed, and nothing very terrible happened. Kelly made fun of Martha and Ivy, all right, but always from enough distance to make it possible to ignore it; and Ivy seemed willing to ignore it if she had a chance. And of course, Martha was willing— more than willing. Things went quickly back to the old pattern of Martha and Ivy and no one else.

Martha and Ivy were meeting again at Bent Oaks Grove after school and on weekends. The first few times they did nothing but talk, sitting in Falcon's Roost or stretched out on the ledge above the cave. Sometimes Josie was with them, and sometimes she wasn't. Josie was almost six now and in first grade, and Ivy no longer had to take her everywhere she went. But she still loved to come to Bent Oaks Grove, and she still was fun to play with. For a few days Ivy and Martha had a good time giving Josie climbing lessons.

Ivy, who had grown up in the woods around Harley's Crossing, said she could have climbed all the way to the Doorway at Josie's age, and it was too bad that city living had put Josie so far behind. So the lessons started, and in a few days Josie could climb almost all the way to the Lookout. Josie was good at climbing, and she was very happy about all the attention. The only thing she wanted more of was the Tree People Game.

Josie remembered an amazing amount about the Tree People, considering how young she had been at the time, and she kept begging Martha and Ivy to play it again.

"Now let's do about the Tree People," she kept saying.

"Okay," Ivy would say. "We're going to. We just have to do—this—or that—or something else—first."

Martha felt the same way. She would have liked to play the Tree People Game, but somehow she never could quite begin.

One afternoon when Josie wasn't there, she decided to bring it out in the open. "Why *don't* we play the Tree People Game?" she said to Ivy.

"We will," Ivy said quickly. "We're going to. We just haven't been in the right mood yet."

"Maybe that's it," Martha said. "We just haven't been in the right mood." Ivy was frowning, so Martha smiled at her and started twisting up in the rubber tire swing she was sitting in. She went around and around until the rope was tight and then let go and spun madly. When it stopped, feeling a little giddy and careless, she asked, "How do you think we're doing— with the spell, I mean? Do you think we're really getting any younger?"

Ivy didn't answer. She was lying in the warm dry grass at the edge of the grove. Martha waited, but

Ivy still didn't answer so she crawled out of the swing and went to sit beside her. "Are you really sure you don't ever want to grow up?" Martha asked.

Without raising her head Ivy said, "I'm *sure*. I'm very sure. Aren't you?"

"Well," Martha said, wishing she could see Ivy's face before she answered. "I don't know. Sometimes it seems like it might be fun to be just a little older."

"How old?" Ivy asked in a muffled voice.

"Oh, I don't know. But it seems as if Cath and Tom are a pretty good age. At least, they seem to be having a lot of fun."

"How old are they?"

"Tom is fifteen, and Cath is almost seventeen."

Ivy shook her head, rocking her face on her arm. "That's *way* too late," she said finally.

Martha sighed, and suddenly Ivy raised her head with a jerk to show her Carson face, hard and angry. "Okay," she said. "Go ahead and cop out if you want to. Grow up. I don't care." She sat up, whirling around so that her back was to Martha. She sat straight and still with her head held stiffly high.

After a while Martha said, "I do care, Ivy. I don't want to—cop out. I just wonder—sometimes."

Ivy's shoulders went down a little, and she turned around. She smiled, but it was a strange smile, more frightening than her anger. "Okay," she said. "I know you were just wondering. It's just that—well, maybe you can grow up if you want to. I can't."

18

SEVERAL TIMES MARTHA CAME CLOSE TO ASKING IVY what she meant that day when she said she couldn't grow up. But she didn't ask because she kept getting the feeling that the answer would be something she didn't want to hear. So she only worried, without asking—and she might have worried longer if something important hadn't happened to take her mind off it.

What happened began as an announcement that there were to be drama classes at Rosewood Junior High. Rosewood had never had anything more than class plays before, but now there was to be a big musical in the spring with a real drama teacher, borrowed from the high school, in charge. Anyone in junior high could try out, but some of the musicians and technicians were going to be brought in from Roosevelt High.

The announcement was made at a regular Friday afternoon assembly. The Rosewood principal, Mr. Gregory, introduced a pretty young woman who turned out to be the high school drama teacher, Miss Walters. Then Miss Walters explained all about how people could go about signing up for drama instead of study hall if they were interested, and how the tryouts would be conducted. She was very enthusiastic and amusing, and she talked a lot about what a professional production the musical was going to be. It seemed that nearly all the eighth grade girls were very much interested in dramatics, especially when they heard that high school boys would be helping out with the technical things.

Martha was one of the few who wasn't. She was only half-listening, amusing herself by watching the excited bouncing and whispering going on in Kelly's group a few rows in front of her, when Ivy tapped her arm.

"Let's sign up," Ivy mouthed. Martha was dumbfounded.

"Us?" Martha whispered. "You and me? What for?"

"For a part."

Because it was so far from being a possibility in Martha's mind, she answered stupidly, "A part of what?"

Ivy laughed. "A part in the play, silly." She saw a teacher looking at them and put her finger in front of her lips. "Shhh. I'll tell you later."

She did, but it took a lot of telling before Martha was convinced. It seemed there were many reasons. The first was that Ivy had a strong feeling that Martha would be good at acting.

"Me?" Martha said. "Me? Why?"

"Because you're so good at being other people. Like Queen Oleander, for instance. Remember how great you were at being Queen Oleander?"

"Yes, but that was different. No one was watching except you and Josie."

"It's not different, not really. You can get used to the rest of it, the audience and everything. But the other part—the really being someone else—you either have or you don't. Some people are only good at being themselves, and that's all they'll ever be good at. They're just born that way."

"Well, I certainly wasn't born *that* way," Martha said. "But I'm not sure I was born the other way either. What's the other reason?"

"Well," Ivy said, "there's going to be dancing in the play." And that was all she needed to say about that.

Another reason was that Ivy suspected Miss Walters might be another secret un-grown-up, like Mrs. Smith. Not that she had any proof, but there was the bouncy way Miss Walters moved around, and the way

168

she got so excited about everything.

"She does seem nice," Martha said doubtfully. With so many reasons arrayed against her, it hardly seemed worth arguing, but she agreed with very strong misgivings. Of course, Ivy was usually right about things, even things she had no way of knowing about. And the idea of acting a part on a stage was so unexpectedly intriguing that Martha could almost make herself believe she would be able to do it. That is, she could almost make herself believe it half of the time, and the rest of the time she just worried.

So Martha and Ivy signed up for the play and started attending drama class, but in the meantime the worries continued to hover like dark clouds in the back of Martha's mind. She tried to ignore them, but she knew they were there—dark and heavy, and filled with lightning waiting the right time to strike. And Martha couldn't help feeling that being in the play was, somehow, inviting the lightning—like flying a kite in a thunderstorm.

The drama class started with a short study of acting techniques and stage terminology and classroom improvisations. Martha managed to get through her improvisation with only minor panic, and she felt great about it afterwards. It was about that time something important began to develop in Bent Oaks Grove.

Josie was still begging for the Tree People, and suddenly it all became possible again by making the whole thing into a play. The story of the Tree People became a serialized dramatic production, like an outdoor soap opera, with daily sequences performed for a small but enthusiastic audience.

Martha and Ivy rebuilt the old flooring in the shallow cave for a stage, collected props and costumes and organized all the best moments in the history of the Tree People into scenes. And it was more fun than ever.

Costuming was no problem. Ivy was able to bring all sorts of strange and exotic articles of clothing from the endless clutter of the Carson house; and what she couldn't find, Martha could usually rescue from the forgotten depths of closets in the Abbotts' household. Special costumes were developed for each of the important characters in the play. Prince Willow, for example, always wore a short cape made from an old Spanish shawl, and a plumed hat fashioned from a round velvet sofa cushion with most of the stuffing removed and decorated with a peacock feather pinned on with a large phony-diamond pin. It was important that each character have a specific costume, since Ivy and Martha were the only actors. Otherwise, it would have been necessary for them to mar the realism of every entrance by stopping to announce who they were at that particular moment.

Martha's specialties turned out to be the highly dramatic parts, including, of course, the sinister Queen Oleander. As a matter of fact, Martha's Queen Oleander soon became a real masterpiece of menacing evil, and by far the favorite character of an enthusiastic audience of Bent Oaks theatergoers. And very soon that wasn't just Josie, either. It wasn't long before some of the young children who came to Bent Oaks from time to time found out about the plays and became regular patrons. And by the time they'd started bringing some friends, an audience of eight or ten little kids wasn't unusual.

Martha, the actress, was a real and honest amazement to Martha, the Mouse, but Ivy professed to be not the least bit surprised.

"I knew you'd be good at it," she said. That made Martha feel even more confident, somehow. But it didn't explain why she could act when giving a talk to the class on even a two-minute current event, had always meant horrible sleepless nights, full of waking nightmares about stupid mistakes or even complete breakdowns with tears and panic. On the other hand acting, at least once she was on stage and had gotten started, was hardly frightening at all. Not frightening, but wildly exciting, in a way that Martha hadn't been excited about anything in her whole life before.

The Bent Oaks Theater was well-established by the time Miss Walters got around to the tryouts for casting the musical, and Martha signed up to try out for a straight dramatic role—only group singing and no dancing. Of course, Ivy signed up for the lead dancer, and it wasn't until Martha saw the sign-up sheet with Kelly Peters' name in big curly letters, right under Ivy's, that it began to be clear just what form the lightning might take.

The day of the tryouts Martha was thrilled—and horrified—to learn that she had gotten a part. A character part, not too important, but with some real acting in it. And during lunch hour she went, with mixed feelings, to sit in the back of the auditorium and watch the tryouts for the dancing parts. There were eight or ten girls trying out, and Miss Walters began by explaining that since they were not professionals, she was not going to ask them to do any set routines or steps. Instead, she would play a record once while they all listened, and then they would be asked to improvise to the music, one at a time. They were just to move freely to the music, any way it made them feel.

Of course, most of the girls didn't do much more than pose and giggle around the stage. So, when the fourth or fifth contestant had stumbled in pink-faced retreat back to her seat, Kelly Peters' entrance was an electrifying contrast. From the moment she wafted on stage dressed in leotards and real ballet slippers, with her hair pulled back in a floating blond ponytail, it was perfectly plain that she had taken ballet lessons since she was seven years old. As a matter of fact, it began to seem to Martha, after the first dazzle of contrast had begun to wear off, that what Kelly was doing was less a dance than a carefully done series of ballet exercises. It also seemed to Martha that what Kelly was doing had very little relationship to the music, as if she had decided on the steps she would do and the order in which she would do them before she even heard Miss Walters' record.

But, Martha told herself, she was probably prejudiced. It certainly was obvious that the rest of the audience was very favorably impressed. When Miss Walters lifted the needle from the record, all the other contestants and watchers sighed and clapped and nodded to each other that, of course, Kelly had won the part.

Then it was Ivy's turn. As Martha watched her walk to the wings, she felt almost more nervous and shaky than she had for her own tryout. Ivy walked slowly to the middle of the stage and waited there for the music to start. She had unbraided her hair, and it foamed around her thick and curly. Coming right after Kelly's pink roundness, Ivy looked startlingly wild and thin and dark. The music started, but Ivy went on standing, staring down at her bare feet, until Martha in agony, thought perhaps she was frozen with stage fright—and then she began.

The music started out light and bright, and Ivy moved in a swinging skip, as if she were going through a field of flowers on a beautiful morning. As the music became freer and wilder, Ivy pranced and gamboled, tossing her black mane of hair, whirling and leaping like a crazy thing. Finally the dance slowed and softened with the music and at last swayed sadly into stillness.

Martha watched the girls in the audience look at each other uncertainly, with surprised faces. One or two of them burst into applause and then quickly stopped.

Martha knew that Ivy had not danced real ballet, as Kelly had. But it seemed to Martha that Ivy had danced the music so exactly that you felt what she did as much with your ears as with your eyes. She had danced the music, and the way it made her feel, and the way she felt about dancing. It had seemed beautiful to Martha, but she didn't know if anyone else thought so—at least she didn't know until she looked at Miss Walters.

Looking at Miss Walters' face, Martha immediately knew that Ivy had won the part of the lead dancer; and a moment later, looking at Kelly Peters' face, Martha also knew that there was going to be trouble.

Martha stayed around long enough to hear the parts announced—Ivy Carson, the lead dancer, and Kelly in the chorus along with five of the others. After the announcement, Miss Walters called the dancers up on the stage to talk to them. The bell had rung, and Martha couldn't wait any longer for Ivy so she started to leave. Outside the auditorium, she passed a small group of Kelly's closest friends, who stopped talking to stare at her. Then Debbie Ralston broke away from the group and ran after her. Martha walked faster, but Debbie caught up and grabbed her arm.

"What did you and Ivy do to get Miss Walters to give you the parts you wanted?" she said.

"Wha-what did we do?" Martha said. "Nothing. Just what she told us to."

"Oh sure," Debbie said. "And that's why she picked Ivy even though Kelly was a thousand times better. That makes a lot of sense. I'll bet you gave Miss Walters some big sob story about how 'poor Ivy' should have the part because her family's a bunch of drunks and jailbirds."

It was Debbie talking, but it sounded like Kelly's style and vocabulary. Martha jerked her arm away and ran down the hall, but not fast enough to keep from hearing, "You and Ivy are going to get called out."

At Rosewood Junior High, being "called-out" was usually just talk—mostly used by boys and most often forgotten by the time the day was over. It was unusual when you heard about some determined boys who actually met after school to fight. Coming from a girl it was even more unusual, and frightening. A girl would have to be much angrier to consider such a thing, and a girl was less apt to mean a fair fight, one against one. Kelly probably had in mind a kind of mass attack.

There was no chance to talk to Ivy until after school, so Martha had to suffer through two hours, pretending to think about social studies and art. What would she do, she kept thinking? How would she face it? How could she possibly face a real fight with scratching and hair pulling? And what if she ran away and left Ivy to face it alone, or did something else as terrible?

After school, Martha ran to meet Ivy in front of her locker and got there just in time to see Ivy pulling a rolled up slip of paper out of the locker handle. The paper said, "You two creeps are CALLED-OUT. Today after school." Ivy grinned at Martha, wadded the paper up and threw it in the trash can.

"What shall we do?" Martha said, trying not to sound as desperate as she felt.

Ivy shrugged. "We won't do anything," she said. "The whole thing is just stupid."

"Do you know who wrote it?" Martha asked. "And why?"

"Kelly, I guess," Ivy said, opening her locker and putting away her books. "And I know what it's about, of course. But not why. I don't really see why, at least not exactly."

"It's because you won the dancing part," Martha said. "And Kelly wanted it."

"I *know* that," Ivy said. "I know that's what it's *about*. But that's not why. I mean people don't just automatically get beat up because they win a dancing part. Not that I've ever heard of."

In spite of herself, Martha laughed a little. "No, I guess not," she said. "I guess the 'why' is just who Kelly is—and who she *thinks* she is. Like the Queen of Rosewood Junior High, or something."

But Ivy didn't laugh with Martha. Instead her face tightened and she said, "Or else it's who I am. A lot of it is just who Ivy *Carson* is."

Things Martha wanted to say ran through her mind. She wanted to say, "That has nothing to do with it," but she knew that probably wasn't true. And also she wanted to say, "Please, Ivy. Don't talk that way." But instead she only said, "They'll probably be waiting for us on the way home. A whole lot of them."

"Then we'll go home some other way," Ivy said.

"But if we do that, they'll tell everybody and say we're cowards."

"So what?" Ivy said. "People say all sorts of stupid things."

Martha's hands started twisting together. "But— but my father says that anybody who runs away from a fight can't ever look himself in the face again."

That made Ivy grin again. "Well, if he said *him*self, he couldn't have been talking about you," she said. "Besides, my Aunt Evaline always says that fighting never solves anything."

Martha nodded, thinking that that sounded pretty true, but also thinking that not fighting left some things to be solved, too. At least right at the moment.

"But how are we going to get home?" she said.

"Easy. We'll go out behind the auditorium and climb the fence instead of going out the gate. And then we'll go home in a big circle. By tomorrow, they'll probably have forgotten all about it."

The grounds of Rosewood Junior High were entirely enclosed in a high chain-link fence that was not at all easy to climb because the links were too small to provide good footholds. However Ivy pointed out that if you were barefooted, some good toeholds were possible. Therefore it was only necessary to take off your shoes and socks and throw them over the fence before you started over.

Ivy reached the other side very quickly, but as Martha started down the outside of the fence, her skirt got hung up on the sharp wire ends that fringed the top. Ivy was on her way back up to help unhook the skirt, when Mr. Gregory, the principal of Rosewood Junior High came around the corner of the building.

"All right, young ladies, what's going on here?" His tone of voice was not exactly angry, but it was definitely cool.

Martha and Ivy stared at him, clinging to the outside of the fence like a couple of paralyzed monkeys, immobilized with apprehension. "We—we were just climbing the fence," Ivy finally managed.

"That much is fairly obvious," Mr. Gregory said. "But since there are rules about climbing the fence, and since the front gate is still wide open, it might be more interesting to hear *why* you are climbing the fence."

"We were just taking a short cut," Martha blurted.

Ivy actually grinned. "Well, more of a long cut."

The grin seemed to help. Mr. Gregory smiled, too. Or at least he twitched in a way that suggested a smile.

"Well, may I suggest that you get down off the fence and enter the school yard in the proper manner —by the gate."

"You mean, we have to come to your office?" Martha's voice quavered, and she felt her eyes begin to flood.

"Oh no," Mr. Gregory said rather hastily. "I don't think that will be necessary. I was just suggesting that if you want to go back on the school grounds, you should do it in the usual way."

Martha realized then that Mr. Gregory had only seen her motionless at the top of the fence, and Ivy climbing back up, and had assumed they were on their way in.

"Oh," she breathed in relief. "But we were going the other way. We were just going home."

"You were leaving?" Mr. Gregory sounded a little incredulous. "You didn't appear to be leaving."

"We really were, though," Ivy said.

Mr. Gregory sort of threw up his hands. "Very well, then leave," he almost snapped, and Martha and Ivy skidded down the fence without even stopping to feel for toeholds, grabbed their shoes, and ran.

19

AFTER A LONG, TENSE AND ROUNDABOUT JOURNEY, Martha and Ivy reached Castle Court without seeing anything of Kelly and her gang. Martha guessed that Kelly's ambush was probably still waiting for them just outside the school gates, but Ivy seemed to think it had all been nothing more than an empty threat.

"They probably weren't even looking for us," she said. "They probably only wanted to scare us."

Martha wasn't so sure. "Maybe they're up on the hill waiting for you when you go up the path," she said.

"I doubt it," Ivy said. "But I'll go a different way, just in case. I'll take the cutoff down to the freeway and around." She started off up the sidewalk, turning once to look back and wave. Martha stood at the beginning of her own sidewalk, close enough to the front door to be sure that no one could cut her off from it, and watched Ivy go. She held her breath as Ivy disappeared around the corner of the Peters' house, and breathed again when she reappeared farther up the hill. She looked tiny and alone. Martha's fists clenched, and she actually took a few steps to run after Ivy and offer to walk her part way home. But then she stopped and reminded herself how little help she'd probably be if something did happen, and went inside and closed the door instead.

The next morning before school, there was a knock on the door, and when Martha opened it, there stood Kelly Peters. Martha was fairly surprised to see her, but she was even more surprised at her own reaction.

"Hello Kelly, what do you want?" she said, sounding, and even feeling, amazingly cool.

Kelly smiled her most candied smile. "May I come in?" she asked sweetly.

In the entry hall, Kelly got right to the point. "Look, Martha, I'm not really mad at *you*," she said. "After all, we've been friends since we were only three years old." Her face sharpened. "It's that Ivy Carson I'm going to—" Suddenly the dimples were back. "Oh hellooo, Tom."

Tom was hurrying towards the front door wearing his dirty practice uniform and carrying his helmet. He stopped just long enough to say, "Hi Kelly. Bye Marty." But that was long enough for Kelly to get between him and the door.

"Is the team practicing before school again?" she asked, fluttering and dimpling.

Tom grinned. "Well, actually, I'm on my way to church," he said. "I just dress this way to get attention." Then he tucked his helmet under his arm like a football and pretended to do an end run around Kelly to get to the door. Kelly didn't try to tackle him, but she looked as if she'd like to. She stood at the door and looked after him adoringly for all of thirty seconds before she got back to business.

"I just came to tell you," she said, "that it's that sneak, Carson, that I'm mad at, not you." She smiled winningly. "Okay?"

But Martha did not smile and answer, "Okay." Instead, she said very deliberately, "Okay, what?"

Kelly sighed sharply as if Martha was being very dense. "Okay, you drop Carson, and we're friends again."

Martha had observed and wondered at fits of temper all her life, without ever being able to produce anything like a real one herself—at least not at anything that was capable of returning the feeling. But now, suddenly, she was gloriously, sincerely angry.

"Kelly Peters, you're not my friend and you never have been. You're a PHONY. (That was a word Martha had thought of using to Kelly at least a hundred times.) And if you think I don't know why you want to be my friend all of a sudden, you're crazy, besides."

Kelly stared at Martha, and Martha stared back, feeling almost as astonished as Kelly looked, but at the same time exhilarated, as if she'd finally accomplished something she'd been wanting to do for years. It wasn't until Kelly had stomped out the door that she began to feel more like herself—a little frightened. There was no telling what would happen now.

But the next few days went by uneventfully. And when the weekend came, Ivy and Martha spent part of it at Bent Oaks Grove, keeping a sharp lookout all the time and being careful to stay out of the trees. They were fairly certain that no one in Kelly's gang could climb as they could, but it would be a bad place to be trapped. However, no one came except the usual bunch of little kids, who of course wanted to see another play.

They made up a new play that weekend, and it was a great success. In the play Ivy was a dancing maiden in the court of Queen Oleander. She had to dance in a contest with the Queen's daughter, Princess Mistletoe. The winner, who was to be picked by a Magic Mirror of Truth, was to be the bride of the rightful ruler, handsome Prince Willow. Ivy danced the parts of both the contestants, and the audience got to play the part of the Magic Mirror. The little kids loved the play so much they wanted Martha and Ivy to do it all over again the next day.

On Sunday evening, no one was at home at the Abbotts' except Martha, so Ivy came over for a while.

She stayed until Cath came home, and then Martha walked with her as far as the hill path. The next morning Martha and Ivy left for school at their usual time and went by their usual route. It was the first time they had done that since the "calling-out" and Martha was a little jumpy, but nothing happened until they reached the school grounds. And then she forgot all about Kelly, caught up in a mysterious general excitement that became apparent the moment they reached the school gates.

It was immediately obvious that something out of the ordinary was going on. Kids were milling around the teachers' parking lot excitedly, and there was a police car parked near the office entrance. It didn't take long to pick up some of the rumors that were flying around.

It seemed that sometime during the weekend someone had broken into the school office and torn everything up. A window had been broken, and the latch unfastened. Inside, everything was a mess. Desks were tipped over, ink was poured over everything, and everything breakable was smashed. Ivy and Martha were still listening to different versions of what had happened and who had probably done it, when Mr. Gregory came out of his office, looking very grim, and ordered everyone to get out of the office area and report to their first period classes.

At noon that day, Kelly and some of her gang sat directly behind Martha and Ivy in the cafeteria; but except for some whispering and a few sneaky glances, nothing at all unusual happened. It was that afternoon, during sixth period, that Martha and Ivy were called to the principal's office.

On the way to Mr. Gregory's office, Martha and Ivy wondered a little uneasily what was up—but they never even came close to expecting the truth. When Mr. Gregory took them into his office, closed the door and told them that he had good reason to believe that they had been responsible for the vandalism in the main office, they both just sat and stared at him as if they had been stricken dumb. And, then, before they had a chance to recover, he went on to say that before they said anything, he wanted them to know that several of their classmates had overheard them talking about how they had done it.

Suddenly Ivy gasped, looked at Martha, and said, "Kelly. Kelly Peters." Of course, Ivy was thinking of Kelly sitting near them in the cafeteria, whispering and looking in their direction and probably plotting to accuse Martha and Ivy at that very moment. But to Mr. Gregory it must have sounded as if Ivy was just realizing that Kelly had been close enough to overhear their incriminating discussion.

When Ivy and Martha were finally given a chance to talk, of course they denied everything; but almost from the first they could see it was useless. When Martha tried to suggest that Kelly was very mad at them, and it was even possible that she had done the vandalism herself in order to blame them for it, Mr. Gregory looked positively horrified.

"Kelly Peters?" he said, shaking his head at Martha sadly, to indicate how low she had sunk to even suggest such a thing. It was fairly plain that Mr. Gregory, like most adults, believed in the angel-faced version of Kelly. "Kelly was away this weekend with her parents. Kelly's father is a friend of mine, and I happen to know they didn't get back to Rosewood 'til quite late Sunday night." He sighed as if he were terribly depressed by so much evil behind such innocent-appearing faces. "You ought to realize, girls," he said, "how very reluctant Kelly was to tell what she had overheard today. Kelly is not the kind of girl to enjoy getting two of her friends into trouble, I'm sure. However she realized that it was clearly her duty to her school and classmates. I'm sure it was a very difficult decision for her to make." After that speech Martha knew for sure that it was useless.

Next Mr. Gregory went on to make a big thing out of the fact that he had caught them climbing "into" the school grounds not long before. He didn't exactly say so, but it was plain that he felt he had interrupted some kind of dry run—a training exercise for a crime in the planning.

And finally Mr. Gregory began to go into what was going to happen, and at that point Martha, who had until then been amazingly firm and tearless, broke down and cried her usual huge wet tears. She knew it looked bad, as if she had more to cry about than just her old familiar terror and a new outrage at being so falsely accused, but she couldn't help it. If they confessed freely, Mr. Gregory was saying, and if their parents agreed to pay for the damage, perhaps the police would agree to stay out of it. But if not— The rest he only hinted at, but he managed to give an impression of unmentionable horrors—iron bars, chains and rat-infested dungeons.

The session in Mr. Gregory's office ended without an ending. Mr. Gregory, who certainly didn't seem to be great at seeing through people, managed, at least, to see that Ivy and Martha were nowhere near confessing, although it didn't seem to have ever occurred to him that the reason they were being so stubborn was simply that they weren't guilty. But, at last, he gave up trying to get a confession and sent them home for the time being.

They were to go home and tell their parents about what had happened; and when they came to school the next morning, their parents were to come with them. Otherwise, they would not be allowed in school and Mr. Gregory would have to tell their parents and the police, himself.

On their way home Martha cried and then stopped crying long enough to babble about telling her parents and what they might do and say. It must have been the tears that kept her from noticing how long Ivy had been quiet. They were almost to Castle Court when she blinked them away enough to really see Ivy —and then the tears stopped, shocked away in an instant.

Ivy was walking stiffly with her hands clenched at her sides. Her face was clenched, too, like an angry fist closed over something dark and hot that seethed just at the edge of explosion.

"Ivy?" Martha asked uncertainly, and the explosion came. Ivy whirled on Martha with a twisted face. Her voice was not loud, but it sounded like screaming.

"You know why he's so sure," she said. "Why old Gregory's so sure we did it? You know why don't you? It's because of me. He'd never have believed that dirty liar, if I hadn't been a part of it. Or if I'd been someone besides Ivy *Carson*—a jailbird Carson. You can't blame old Gregory, actually. Who else could have done it? After all I'm the only Carson left in his crummy school except Josie, and she's not quite old enough. Not quite, but it won't be long for her either."

Ivy turned her back on Martha and started off, but Martha ran after her.

"Stop, Ivy," she said. "That's not true. That's not true, Ivy."

Ivy stopped. "What's not true about it?"

"Well, it's just not," Martha stammered. "It's not because you're a Carson." Then she grabbed Ivy's arm and smiled a phony smile and said, "Besides, you're not a Carson, remember. You're a changeling."

Ivy jerked away. "Shut up!" she said in a blazing

whisper. "Shut up! I'm no changeling. There's no such thing as a changeling. I was lying to you. I was lying to you all the time—about everything." She whirled and ran furiously toward the hill path, and Martha only stood and watched her go.

Martha went on then, very slowly, and when she got home no one was there as usual. She went into her bedroom and sat stiffly on the edge of the bed for a long time. She just sat there thinking, and by the time the rest of the family got home she'd begun to feel a little better. If her parents believed her and would help her prove that she and Ivy were innocent, then surely everything would be all right. After all, her father was a lawyer, and he should be able to defend his own daughter—even though he was really a business lawyer and didn't usually defend criminals, even innocent ones. But if they didn't believe her, she would have to do something else. She didn't know exactly what she would do, but she'd think about that later if the truth didn't work.

By the time Grandmother Abbott and Martha's father got home, dinner was almost ready, so Martha decided to put off the telling until after dinner. During the meal, Martha found it very hard to swallow, and Grandmother asked her twice why she wasn't eating. The meal seemed to take forever. Tom was eating at a friend's house, but Cath was home and she brought up a topic of conversation that was always good for a long family discussion—whether she was old enough to have her own car. The arguments for and against went on and on and on.

At last the dinner came to an end, and Cath went to her room to study. Grandmother Abbott went into the kitchen, and Martha was left alone with her parents. Three times she started to say, "I have to tell you something," and three times it wouldn't come out. And when it finally did, the pain of saying it must have showed in her face, because her mother and father immediately gave her their full attention. But just then Grandmother Abbott came back into the room, and of course, she stayed to listen.

Martha began at the beginning and told the whole story without too many interruptions. Once Mrs. Abbott asked if anyone *had* talked to Miss Walters about picking Ivy for the dancing part, instead of Kelly.

"No," Martha said. "No one that I know about, anyway. Why?"

"Well it just does seem a little strange, since Kelly has studied dancing for so long, that she wasn't given the lead role. Doesn't it, dear? That is, if the roles were given out on the basis of talent and ability."

Mr. Abbott smiled knowingly. "I'm beginning to think that that wasn't the basis," he said. "It seems to me that this Miss Walters must see herself as something of a therapist, instead of strictly a drama coach. I suppose it's a valid approach to theater at this level. A bit hard on audiences, however. And a bit hard on the kids who lose out. And if that *is* the case, your

Miss Walters should, at least, have made it clear to the ones who missed out, through no fault of their own. If you're going to take something away from a kid who's earned it to give it to someone who needs it more, you should at least tell the loser the real reason."

Martha found that she was breathing very hard, and it wasn't just from fear, anymore. "For your information, Dad," she said. "For your information, the reason Ivy got the part was because she was the best. And I know you won't believe it, but that was the reason I got the part I tried out for, too."

Mr. Abbott stared at Martha for a moment, and then he grinned. "Good for you, Marty. It's good to see you stand up and fight for once. But I really wasn't referring to you—not for a minute. I wouldn't want you to think that."

When Martha got to the part of her story about the vandalism and Kelly's accusation, everybody stopped grinning. Martha just barely got to the end of what Mr. Gregory had said without tears, but when Grandmother Abbott said, "Now tell us the absolute truth, dear. You know we'll stand by you no matter what?" she began to cry.

"I told you," she sobbed. "We didn't have anything to do with it."

"When did it happen? The vandalism?" Mr. Abbott asked.

"I don't know for sure. Mr. Gregory asked us about

Saturday and Sunday night both, so I guess he's not sure either. I guess no one is at the school at all on Sunday, so no one would have seen it until Monday morning either way."

"Well, your grandmother was here at home with you Saturday evening, so we're all right there," Mr. Abbott said. "And Cath was home with you last night, wasn't she?"

"No," Martha said slowly. "Cath didn't get home until later. Ivy was here at the house with me until Cath came home. That was about nine or maybe ten. I didn't notice. Before that Ivy and I did some homework, and then we played some records and Ivy danced. We didn't go anywhere. Except I walked a little way with Ivy when she left. But Cath was back by then, and I was only gone a few minutes. Cath can tell you that, I think. That is, if she noticed."

For a long time no one said anything, and then Grandmother Abbott said, "Of course, you don't know for sure if Ivy went directly home when she left you, Martha."

Martha looked at her parents. Her father said, "That's right, Mouse, you really have no way of knowing what happened after that. You say it was a little before ten o'clock."

Martha stood up and walked out of the room, only shaking her head in answer to their calls for her to come back. She couldn't have answered if she'd wanted to. In her room she lay down on the bed with her face in the pillow.

In a few minutes Martha's mother came into the room with a cold wet washcloth for her face.

"You stay right there for now, dear," she said. "Your father had to run out for just a minute. He promised Mr. Simmons he'd drop over for a few minutes this evening to discuss some tax problem, but he said to tell you he'd be right back. In the meantime you should try to relax. And don't worry, dear. We know that whatever happened, our little Marty just couldn't have been to blame."

"Oh Mother," Martha said and started crying all over again.

Her mother left then, and it was sometime later that there was another knock on the door and Tom stuck his head in.

"Hey Marty," he said, "have you seen my— Hey, what's going on?"

"Nothing," Martha sobbed. "Go away."

But Tom didn't go away. He came over and stood by the bed. He stood there shuffling around for a while, and then he patted Martha's shoulder, which made her cry harder than ever.

"Tell me, Marty," he said. "What is it?"

"I can't. Go ask them. They'll tell you."

"Okay. Okay," Tom said. "But take it easy. It can't be that bad." And he went away.

Sometime, not too long after that, Martha cried herself into a very sound sleep. Much later she was vaguely aware of someone coming in and taking her shoes off and covering her up. The next thing that happened was a new day.

Martha woke up slowly and reluctantly, knowing that she'd rather not wake up before she was able to remember why. Then she realized that she was still wearing her clothes from the day before, and it all came back in a great suffocating wave.

When Martha hurried into the dining room a few minutes later, everyone else was already there. All of them, all the Abbotts, were sitting around the table— her father and mother, Grandmother Abbott, Cath and Tom. For a moment they all looked at her without saying anything, but even before they spoke Martha knew that something had made a very great difference.

20

THAT DAY, THE NEXT DAY AFTER MARTHA AND IVY were accused by Kelly, was a time that no one in the Abbott family would ever forget. When Martha walked into the dining room that morning, all the rest of them already knew something that made a very great difference. Martha heard about it later in bits and pieces.

She heard that after Tom had found her crying, he had gone to the kitchen, where his mother and grandmother were, and asked what was the matter with the Mouse. So Mrs. Abbott explained, trying to make it sound not too serious so as not to worry Tom, who was always too quick to get caught up in everyone else's problems. When she finished the story, she said, "We don't really think that Martha was involved, but

197

if it turns out that she was, it should be easy to prove that she was very little to blame. She has never been in any trouble in her life except when she was under the influence of that Carson child. It's very much our fault for not being more firm about ending the relationship."

Tom hadn't said a word while Mrs. Abbott was talking, but his face had looked more and more strange; and when she had finished, he suddenly reached out and snatched a dishtowel and bowl out of his mother's hands and threw them across the room with all his might. The bowl smashed into the refrigerator with a great shattering crash, and Tom turned and stalked into the living room and sat there, silent and glowering, refusing to speak to anybody until his father came home from the Simmons'.

Then Tom told all of them about what had really been happening. He started by explaining that one of his friends, Brent Hardison, whose parents had been bridge friends of the Abbotts for years, was a pusher.

"A pusher," Tom said impatiently, when his father asked him what on earth he thought he was talking about. "A pusher. A dope peddler. He buys grass and speed and acid in the city, and he sells them at school. He's been doing it for months."

Then Tom went on to say that on Saturday night he and two other guys had some pills that one of the guys got from Brent. Tom wasn't sure what they were. Maybe speed, maybe not. Tom hadn't taken much stuff like that before, and he didn't know too much about it. Anyway when the effects began to wear off, they decided that they wanted to buy some more, but they were all broke by then—all three of them. They were in one of the guys' cars, parked down on Warwick near the Junior High, and all of a sudden Tom remembered that when he was in school there, he was the one who took the cafeteria money to the office, because he was such a good reliable boy. And he had seen where the secretary always put it, along with the money from all the other rooms, in the drawer of her desk.

Because they were still feeling strange from the pills, Tom couldn't remember all the details too clearly, but he did remember that when it turned out there wasn't any money in the drawer, they had all gotten angry and smashed things up a little. Then they had climbed back out the window and gone home.

The earthquake that shook the Abbotts' house that night had aftershocks that went on shaking for a long time. Tom and the two other boys who had broken into the school were not sent away to jail or reform school as Martha had feared that she would be. Instead, after their fathers had paid for the damage, they were only put on probation, for a long time; and Tom and the one other boy who also played football were kicked off the team. Brent Hardison, though, spent a long time in Juvenile Hall and then was sent away to a boarding school by his family.

Tom signed up for some art classes to fill the gap in his schedule that football had left, and the adult Abbotts all talked about how bravely he had made the adjustment, with no morbidness or complaints. But Tom told Martha that when he said he really didn't mind, he meant it.

That very big difference that Martha sensed that morning when she walked into the dining room never entirely went away. It came and went, and changed in various ways—but things were never quite the same in the Abbotts' house after that. The most important change, as far as Martha could see, was that the Abbotts listened to each other. Not that they always understood each other, or even agreed with each other much more. But it seemed to Martha that after that day, everyone tried a little harder to listen.

A smaller difference that happened soon after that day was that the Abbotts and their next door neighbors, the Peters, stopped speaking to each other for a while. A few days after everything happened, Mr. Abbott went over to talk to the Peters. By then the whole neighborhood was talking about what Tom and his friends had done, but apparently no one was talking about the lie that Kelly had told. During the course of the conversation, Mr. Abbott asked Mr. Peters if he knew about the accusation that Kelly had made concerning Martha and Ivy. And Mr. Peters said quickly that he did know about it, and that Kelly had explained it to him and his wife, and to Mr. Gregory, by the way, to everyone's complete satisfaction.

Kelly, he said, had explained that it wasn't a lie. That she *had* heard Martha and Ivy talking about the break-in—*as if* they had done it. Afterwards Kelly realized that the girls had only been pretending—the way those two were always doing. Just playing one of their games of make-believe. But at the time Kelly hadn't doubted the truth of what she had overheard.

So it was Kelly's word against Martha's, and Mr. Abbott left the Peters without saying any more about it; but when he got home he told Tom. So Tom asked Martha and, of course, Martha told him that it wasn't true. She and Ivy had talked about the play that noon hour, and a little about what Kelly and her friends were up to, with all their whispering. But they hadn't even discussed the break-in, let alone pretended that they had done it.

The next Saturday Tom was out in front of the Abbotts' house washing the car when Kelly and a bunch of her friends came up the street. Martha was sitting on the windowseat in her room, and she saw them coming and wondered what would happen. Tom was barefoot and wearing denim cutoffs. He was still tan from a summer of surfing and his blond hair, streaked by the sun, was lighter than his skin, and his football muscles bulged under his T shirt. He had certainly never looked handsomer, and Martha was pretty sure Kelly's gang of eighth grade boy-worshippers couldn't resist him; and she was right. They couldn't. Instead of going into the Peters' house, they giggled over to watch the car washing.

Even though Martha opened her window a crack, she couldn't hear everything that was being said. The six girls squealed and laughed and pushed each other, each trying to get closest to where Tom was working. Finally Ginny Davis grabbed the rag out of the bucket and started to help wash the car. Immediately the others began to fight over the rag, tearing off pieces, so that they could help, too. But when Kelly got a piece, Tom straightened up from the hubcap he was scrubbing and took the rag firmly out of Kelly's hands.

"Not you, Dimples," he said coldly. "I don't let liars wash my car."

Kelly stared at Tom for a second before she turned and stomped home. Halfway there she stopped and called to her friends, and they started to put down their rags. But Tom grinned at them and said, "You mean I'm going to lose all my slaves?" and so they all stayed, washing and then waxing, and flirting for over an hour. After that the Peters stopped talking to the Abbotts for quite a while.

One of the best differences after that fateful day was the one that involved just Tom and Martha. Tom had always been nice to Martha, in the way that he was nice to nearly everybody; but he had always been too busy to spend much time with her. But after that spring, they began to really talk to each other. They talked about things that Martha had never talked about to anyone except Ivy, and also about things that really mattered to Tom. Some of the things she found out about Tom were a surprise to Martha.

One thing that surprised Martha was the way Tom talked about his art classes. He told Martha that he had always wanted to take art, but he'd never had the time before with so many hours of sports and courses that were required for college. Martha knew that Tom could draw well, but she'd never thought about him being really interested in art. It was a surprise to her to think about Tom wanting to take art and not being able to, because she'd always thought of Tom and Cath both as being able to do anything and everything they ever wanted to. There were other things that Tom told her that surprised her. For instance, he told her once that he was glad, in a way, that Kelly had accused Martha of the vandalism at Rosewood Junior High.

When Martha asked why on earth he was glad about a thing like that, he said because it had trapped him into deciding something for himself. Before that, he said, he'd pretty much just gone along doing what was expected of him—partly because he was just the "why-not" type and partly because he'd always felt he really didn't have much choice. He'd gotten in the habit of going along with whoever was leaning on him hardest at the time. And then that night it dawned on him all of a sudden that when things had gone so far that a couple of harmless kids like Martha and Ivy could get the blame for a crazy thing like what happened to the school office—then it was about time somebody started telling things straight no matter who got hurt. The getting hurt part bothered him, though. He hated the idea of being a fink and getting his friends busted. But when he'd stopped to think about it, he'd known they were going to get busted sooner or later, no matter what. And maybe sooner was better than later. Anyway, Tom said, he was glad that for once in his life he'd done something that *he'd* decided to do—all by himself.

Although the differences at the Abbotts' after that terrible Monday, were, for the most part, more good than bad; there was one very important difference that was bad, all bad. Ivy was gone again.

On that morning, the one after Martha had cried herself to sleep without knowing about Tom's confession, everyone had tried to get in touch with Ivy and the Carsons to tell them what had happened; but no one could reach them. Finally it became apparent that some time in the middle of the night the Carsons had packed up and climbed into their old red truck and disappeared. Everyone thought it was certainly too bad that they had gone off that way, without even knowing the truth about what had happened; but soon nearly everyone forgot about it. After all, everyone said, the Carsons were always coming and going, anyway. Undoubtedly, they'd have left soon, even without the accusation against Ivy; and they'd probably be back someday, and then everything could be straightened out.

But Martha couldn't just forget about it like everyone else. She went over and over what might have happened when Ivy told her parents. Martha was certain that the Carsons hadn't believed that Ivy was innocent. After all, nearly all the other Carson kids had been guilty at one time or another, so why not Ivy? Because, of course, the Carsons didn't understand, any more than anyone else did, about how Ivy was so different.

Another thing that Martha couldn't forget—never, as long as she lived—was the way she and Ivy had parted. To Martha that was the most terrible part of all. She went over her last conversation with Ivy at least a thousand times, wishing she hadn't said what she had about a changeling, wishing she'd run after Ivy until she caught her—no matter how long it took or how far she had to go. Wishing she hadn't let Ivy go off without a chance to say good-by or to take back the things she'd said.

Most of the time Martha felt certain that Ivy would have taken them back, if there'd been time. But with her gone, there was no way to find out for sure. So all Martha could do was go over and over the whole thing in her mind, as if somehow it might finally turn out differently.

21

IVY WAS GONE, AND THERE WAS NO WAY TO CHANGE that; but other things went right on changing. Spring came and the big musical, and Martha's small part was padded because she did it so well, until it turned out to be one of the things everyone liked best about the play. The play ran for three weekends, and Martha discovered how great it was to face and work her way through the terror she felt before every performance—to the place where applause, like warm wonderful thunder, told her she had won.

Later, probably because the stage had been such a great discovery, she decided to try to write a play for an English class assignment. It turned out to be a short one-act skit, but good enough to be staged as part of the fund raising assembly put on by the eighth grade class to raise money for the graduation party.

So the eighth grade finished a lot better than Martha had ever expected it would, and summer came and went and high school began. Martha had always hated to think about starting high school. A new school, much larger, much farther from home, and full of new people had always seemed like a terrifying prospect. But somehow it turned out not to be as bad as she expected. For instance, new people turned out to have certain advantages, such as not remembering that Marty Abbott, the tall slim girl with the long blond hair, had once been the fat and silent Marty Mouse of Rosewood School.

At home, at number two Castle Court, things changed too, but only a little. Martha's father was made a full partner in his law firm and started working about an hour longer every day; and Martha's mother won the Spring Tournament Trophy and began to spend an extra day a week on the golf course. Tom went into his Senior year in high school, and Cath went away to college. Grandmother Abbott spent more and more time in Florida since she had gotten interested in raising orchids. Everyone seemed much less worried about Martha, either because there was less to worry about or because they all had less time to do it in.

Martha had less time, too. Weeks and months rushed by for Martha that year, and like the rest of the Abbotts she began to have to keep calendars and schedules. Schedules such as: Tuesday and Thursday afternoons at 4:00—play rehearsal; Wednesday at 3:30—Conservation Club meeting; Saturdays at 10:00—voice lessons in the city.

Summer came and went, mostly in a long trip by automobile across the country with her family, and then right after the beginning of her Sophomore year, Martha met Rufus. It happened because Martha had allowed herself to be signed up for a course in biology. She had signed up, against her better judgment, when she was pressured a bit by a hurried counselor, because biology happened to fit neatly into a hole in Martha's schedule. The counselor was feeling bad because nothing Martha wanted to take would fit, and because there was a long line of kids waiting impatiently to be counseled. So Martha had told herself that, after all, biology was a *life* science and the life part sounded interesting—forgetting that she'd actually stopped believing in science at a rather early age. Forgetting, too, the rumors she'd heard about the kinds of things that went on in laboratory classes. Things like cutting up poor little defenseless creatures in cold blood.

Sure enough, almost immediately the teacher announced that the atrocities would be starting in a week or two, and that same day Martha waited after class to talk about dropping. While she waited, she noticed the frogs in a big glass tank at the back of the classroom. Drawn by a mixture of pity and fascination, she drifted over to stare at the condemned. Most of the victims crouched resignedly on the tank floor, but not all. Just one, a lovely greenish-brown frog with tragic eyes, stood up on his hind legs, rested his chin on his delicate fingers, and looked Martha right in the eye.

"Then he asked me to help him out," Martha told Rufus afterwards.

"He *asked* you to help him out?" Rufus asked. "In so many words?"

"Of course," Martha said grinning. "How else would he ask me?"

"In that case," Rufus said, "I'm glad I helped. I always rescue talking frogs, every time I get the chance."

Martha hadn't known who was helping at first. There had been a small mob of students crowding around, waiting to see the teacher, who was standing only a few feet away, but with his back turned. Martha shoved aside the tank cover, slipped her hand inside, and was slipping it out full of cool damp frog, when the teacher turned around. She put her hands, frog and all, behind her back.

Looking suspicious but uncertain, the teacher walked towards her. "What do you have there, Miss —ah, Miss—"

"Abbott," Martha supplied, stalling for time. "Martha Abbott." Behind her she felt urgent deliberate fingers touching hers, and the frog was gone. She wiped her damp hands on the seat of her skirt and held them out, empty. She didn't find out until later where the frog had gone—to a safe hiding place in Rufus' pocket.

Soon afterwards, Martha dropped biology without regrets, because she'd discovered that Rufus was also in her drama class. Another thing that Martha discovered about Rufus was that he had friends of just about every kind imaginable. Rufus knew and got along with kids from every group, from the "plaid-and-crew cut" set of Kelly Peters and her friends to the shaggy almost dropouts who smoked pot in the school parking lot during lunch hour. Knowing Rufus meant getting to know a lot of other people in a hurry.

By the spring of her Sophomore year, Martha Abbott knew a lot of people, and more important, she'd begun to know who she was in a way she never had before. She knew, for instance, that if you asked nearly anybody at Roosevelt High who Marty Abbott was, they would probably say, "You know, the tall chick who's in all the school plays." Or even, "The cute blonde who's been going around with Rufus Greene lately." It was great—if still a little amazing to Martha —to know that people thought of her that way, instead of—instead of the way she sometimes still felt inside.

Inside—there were still times when some little thing could send Martha sliding back into the kind of quiet panic she had lived with as Marty Mouse Abbott. But those times didn't come often anymore, and they didn't last long. Now that she had learned the way out of the Mousehole, she never stayed in it for long. And even better than getting out of it quickly was not getting in, and the way to do that was to shut the door. Shutting the door on the Mousehole meant shutting the door on a lot of the past—dozens of silly fears, and the lonely comfort of too many tears, and too many sweets, and too many endless daydreams. And maybe it even meant shutting the door on Bent Oaks Grove—and the memory of Ivy Carson.

Martha hadn't meant it to happen. When Ivy first left, she had thought of very little else. She had worried and wondered and written—even though she had no place to send letters to except to Harley's Crossing, where not even Aunt Evaline lived anymore. But time passed and things kept changing and new things began to happen.

So, by the spring of her Sophomore year, it had been a long time since Martha had been to Bent Oaks Grove, and even longer since she had done much thinking about Ivy Carson.

And then, suddenly, it was the seventh of April and Martha knew all day long that something was about to happen. But it wasn't until after dinner that her father calmly announced that the Carsons were back in Rosewood Hills.

22

"Ivy? Ivy? Ivy?" Sitting on the edge of the stage in Bent Oaks Grove, Martha rocked back and forth in time to the whispered question. It was a question all right, a huge question, and the longer Martha sat there, the more she began to realize that the question had a great many parts.

The first part was about who Ivy was. Who was Ivy *now*—now that she was almost sixteen? What would she look like? What would she act like? Who would she be, after all this time? But who had she ever been, really? Who was the small girl with the wild dark hair and fantastic eyes who claimed not to be what everyone thought she was—and had to be?

But the longer Martha thought about it, the more she began to see that there was another important part to the question, and that other part was about Martha Abbott. Who had Martha Abbott been, and who would she be now, if there had never been an Ivy? And what was the feeling that had made Martha's stomach tighten and the blood tingle into her face when she heard that the Carsons had returned? Was it just excitement? Was Martha really just glad that Ivy was back? Or had it been partly fear? Fear of the unknown, and maybe even fear of what it would mean to Marty Abbott—today's Marty Abbott—to have Ivy Carson back in Rosewood Hills? That question was really who Martha Abbott was, and, as usual, Martha didn't entirely believe in the answer.

The shadows deepened in Bent Oaks Grove, and overhead the sky turned a deeper, duller pink, and Martha still waited, and wondered and worried about questions and answers. At last the questions began to turn into daydreams. Something, perhaps the frayed end of a rope dangling where Ivy had hung it years before in Tower Tree, reminded Martha of other times, and pictures began to float up like mirages in front of her eyes.

First there was a face, a small pointed face spinning down a rope, in and out of sunlight. That was when Martha had thought, "Of course, a changeling. That explains everything."

Then there was another Ivy, curled over her bruised foot in the middle of the Smiths' kitchen floor, looking up with glowing eyes, and the Smiths looking down at her with almost startled faces.

Then there was a dim distant Ivy, standing where dark fingers of shadow reached toward her down a hill. That silent ghostly Ivy was just fading when there was a noise of scuffling leaves and a figure moved slowly out of the dark passage between the gateway boulders of Bent Oaks Grove. The figure moved a few steps into the grove and stopped, and Martha caught her breath in a shaky gasp.

Even in the dim light, it was obvious that the person standing so quietly just inside the grove was small, much too small. When she moved forward into the grove, Martha could tell for sure that it was a very little girl. A little girl with long dark hair in heavy braids and thin legs under a short skirt.

It was Ivy. It had to be. But not a sixteen-year-old Ivy. Not even the Ivy Martha had last seen over two years before. This little girl seemed, unbelievably, to be the Ivy of years and years ago.

Crazy impossible explanations flashed through Martha's mind. She sat motionless, staring, with both hands pressed against her mouth, while the shadowy figure stood still, too, with its face turned toward Martha. After an endless time it moved again, forward, and a small quavering voice said, "Martha? Are you Martha?"

Martha jumped to her feet, laughing with relief.

"Josie!" she shouted. "It's Josie."

"Are you Martha?" Josie asked again.

"Yes," Martha said, laughing. "Yes. Don't you know me, Josie?" She ran to Josie and hugged her, but Josie pulled away, staring.

"You look different," she said.

"So do you," Martha said. "I thought you were— I hardly knew you at first. You look just like Ivy."

Josie smiled at that. "I know it," she said. "I *am* just like Ivy."

The night wind was rising now, and suddenly Martha began to shiver. "Why are you here alone, Josie?" she asked. "Where's Ivy?"

Josie's smile drooped. "She's gone away," she said. "She's gone to live in New York."

It was as if a rock, dropped from a great height, had crashed through Martha, landing with a sickening thud somewhere near the bottom of her stomach.

"New York," she said, almost angrily. "She can't go live in New York. She's not even sixteen yet. How could she go to New York?"

Josie looked startled at Martha's reaction, but after a moment she nodded again, firmly. "She did," she said. "She went to learn to be a ballet dancer. See, Aunt Evaline died, and we went to Harley's Crossing because my dad thought that Aunt Evaline was going to give her house and everything to Ivy, and then he could have some of it. But Aunt Evaline's house was sold already, and the money was just for Ivy to go to dancing school. Nobody else could have any of it for anything."

Martha could only nod, struggling against a hot lump in her throat and burning eyes.

"My dad was awful mad," Josie said, looking more cheerful.

"I'll bet," Martha said with a weak giggle. But the giggle was a mistake. Somehow it made a crack in Martha's defenses, and the tears broke through. She turned her back on Josie and walked away. At the edge of the stage she sat down with her face in her hands. She cried for quite a while before she realized that Josie was sitting beside her. She tried to smile at Josie, and then she cried again because she saw that Josie cried the way Ivy used to—silently and without real tears—only with great liquid eyes and wet satin eyelashes.

Finally Josie said, "Ivy says that as soon as she's eighteen, she's going to get her own place to live and I can go live with her. She has to stay with some people Aunt Evaline knew until then. But as soon as she's eighteen, she's going to send for me. Maybe you can go, too."

Martha sighed and smiled at Josie, but she didn't wipe her face. She didn't want to because the tears were for Ivy, and they had been very real and painful.

"Maybe I can," she told Josie. "Anyway, it's great that Ivy's getting to go to ballet school. It's what she wanted more than anything."

Josie nodded. Suddenly she looked around the grove uneasily. "I have to go," she said. "It's almost dark. I have to get home before it's too dark. Goodby." She turned to go and then turned back. "Wait! I almost forgot. I have a letter Ivy wrote for you. She told me to put it in the secret box. That's why I came here—to put it in the secret box." She reached into her pocket and pulled out a crumpled envelope.

"The secret box is right here," Martha said. "I was looking at it just before you came."

"Well, I guess I don't have to put it there, since you're already here," Josie said. She shoved the letter into Martha's hand, hugged her so quickly that Martha barely had time to hug her back, and turned and ran.

The darkness was almost complete, and Martha could barely make out her name written in large letters on the envelope. She started for home, but after a few steps she stopped. Going back for the secret box reminded her of the candles and matches that it held, so she took it instead to the bench at the back of the stage. The first two matches wouldn't strike, but the third one did; and spreading the letter on her knees, she began to read.

Dear Martha,

Tomorrow I'll be in New York, and DANCING, the way I've always wanted to. Aunt Evaline did it all before she died. I'll be living with the people Mrs. W., my old teacher, used to know.

I got the letters you wrote to me a long time

after you wrote them, but they were good let-
ters and I was glad to know that they found out
that we didn't do it. I wanted to write to you
but I couldn't then, and I wanted to come to
Rosewood to see you before New York, but
there wasn't time.

Josie will deliver this letter, and I told her to
look for you sometimes in Bent Oaks. I hope
you still go there. And I hope you can look after
Josie a little until I'm old enough to have her
come stay with me.

I'll write to you, hundreds of letters, when I
get to New York.

Love,

Ivy

P.S. About what I said the day I went away—
about changelings and everything. I guess
you know already I didn't mean it. I know
now I was right about being a changeling.
I had to be. But lots of people are change-
lings, really. You might be one yourself,
Martha Abbott. I wouldn't be surprised.
LOVE—LOVE—LOVE   ivy

Martha folded the letter and put it with the candle
and matches back into the secret box. Then she
climbed up to the hiding place and put the box away.
On the way back down, Martha stopped on the ledge

above the cave.

From the ledge Martha could see way down over Rosewood Manor Estates where the lights were on, now, in most of the houses. The lights were in patterns, square and uniform, window-shaped, and every lighted yard was neatly framed in a dark border of hedge or fence. Around each block the streets made wider boundaries, studded with street lamps like planned and patterned electric stars, for a planned and patterned world.

Further up the hill the lights ended, except for a glow from a strange orange moon that sat just on the edge of the far hills and cast vague restless moonshadows behind every tree and bush. Up there, near the top of the hill, the wind seemed warmer, but much stronger. It rushed in battering gusts against Martha's face and sent her hair flying and whipping behind her head. She raised her face, liking the feel of it. Liking the wild push and pull of the darkness that flowed around her.

After a while she started smiling. "You know what, Martha Abbott?" she said out loud. "I wouldn't be surprised, either."